ANNA CAREY

HARPER

An Imprint of HarperCollins*Publishers*

Eve
Copyright © 2011 by Alloy Entertainment and Anna Carey
All rights reserved. Printed in the United States of America. No part of this book may be used or reproduced in any manner whatsoever without written permission except in the case of brief quotations embodied in critical articles and reviews. For information address HarperCollins Children's Books, a division of HarperCollins Publishers, 10 East 53rd Street, New York, NY 10022.
www.epicreads.com

alloy**entertainment**
Produced by Alloy Entertainment
151 West 26th Street, New York, NY 10001

Library of Congress Cataloging-in-Publication Data
Carey, Anna.
Eve / by Anna Carey. — 1st ed.
    p. cm.
Summary: In 2032, sixteen years after a deadly virus has wiped out most of the earth's population, Eve discovers the terrible fate that awaits students when they graduate from their all-girls school, and she sets off on a treacherous journey into the wilds of The New America, searching for a place where she can survive.
ISBN 978-0-06-204850-9 (tr. bdg.) — ISBN 978-0-06-211418-1 (int'l ed.)
[1. Survival—Fiction. 2. Orphans—Fiction. 3. Science fiction.] I. Title.
PZ7.C21Ev 2011   2011010032
[Fic]—dc22   CIP
                                                                        AC

Design by Liz Dresner
11 12 13 14 15 LP/RRDB 10 9 8 7 6 5 4 3 2 1
❖
First Edition

For my parents

Maybe I really don't want to know what's going on.
Maybe I'd rather not know. Maybe I couldn't bear to know.
The Fall was a fall from innocence to knowledge.

—Margaret Atwood, THE HANDMAID'S TALE

My sweet Eve,

As I drove back from the market today, you humming in your car seat and our trunk filled with powdered milk and rice, I saw the San Gabriel Mountains—really saw them for the first time. I'd taken that road before, but this was different. There they were beyond the windshield: their blue-green peaks still and silent, watching over the city, so close I felt like I could touch them. I pulled over just to look.

I know I will die soon. The plague is taking everyone who was given the vaccine. There are no more flights. There are no more trains. They've barricaded the roads outside of town and now we all must wait. The phones and internet have long since gone out. The faucets are dry and cities are losing power, one by one. Soon the entire world will be dark.

But right now we are still alive. Perhaps more alive than we've ever been. You're sleeping in the next room. From this chair I can hear the sounds

of your music box—the one with the tiny balle-
rina—playing its last few tinkling notes.

I love you, I love you, I love you.
Mom

one

BY THE TIME THE SUN SET OVER THE FIFTY-FOOT PERIM-
eter wall, the School lawn was covered with twelfth-year
students. The younger girls leaned out of the dormitory
windows, waving their New American flags as we sang
and danced. I grabbed Pip's arm and spun her around
when the band played a faster number. Her short, staccato laugh rose above the music.

It was the night before our graduation and we were
celebrating. We'd spent most of our lives inside the compound walls, never knowing the forest beyond it, and this
was the grandest party we'd ever been given. A band was
set up by the lake—a group of eleventh-year girls who'd

volunteered—and the guards had lit torches to keep the hawks away. Laid out on a table were all of my favorite foods: leg of deer, roast wild boar, candied plums, and bowls overflowing with jungle berries.

Headmistress Burns, a doughy woman with a face like a feral dog, was manning the table, encouraging everyone to eat more. "Come on! We don't want to let this go to waste. I want my girls like plump little pigs!" The fat on her arms swung back and forth as she gestured at the spread.

The music slowed and I pulled Pip closer, leading her in a waltz. "I think you make a very good man," she said, as we glided toward the lakefront. Her red hair clung to her sweaty face.

"I *am* handsome," I laughed, furrowing my brow to feign manliness. It was a joke at School, for it had been over a decade since any of us had seen a boy or man, unless you counted the photos of the King that were displayed in the main hall. We begged the teachers to tell us of the time before the plague, when girls and boys attended Schools together, but they only said that the new system was for our own protection. Men could be manipulative, conniving, and dangerous. The one exception was the King. Only he was to be trusted and obeyed.

"Eve, it's time," Teacher Florence called. She stood by the lakefront, a gold medal in her aged, weathered hands. The standard teacher's uniform, a red blouse with blue pants, hung loose on her petite frame. "Gather around, girls!"

The band stopped playing and the air was filled with the sounds of the outside forest. I felt the metal whistle around my neck, thankful to have it should any creature broach the compound wall. Even after all these years at School, I never got used to hearing the dogfights, the distant *rat-tat-tat-tat* of machine guns, the horrible whining of deer being eaten alive.

Headmistress Burns hobbled over and took the medal from Teacher Florence's hand. "Now, now, let us begin!" she cried, as the forty twelfth years lined up to watch. Ruby, our other best friend, stood on her tiptoes to see. "You've all worked very hard during your time at School, and perhaps no one has worked as hard as Eve." She turned to me as she said this. The skin on her face was wrinkled and loose, forming slight jowls. "Eve has proven to be one of the best, brightest students we've taught here. By the power given to me by the King of The New America, I present her with the Medal of Achievement." As Headmistress pressed the cold medallion into my hands, all the girls clapped. Pip added a shrieking finger-whistle for good measure.

"Thank you," I said softly. I glanced across the long, moatlike lake, which stretched from one side of the wall to the other. My gaze settled on the giant windowless building beyond it. The following day, after I gave my valedictory speech in front of the entire school, the guards across the lake would extend a bridge and the graduating class would follow behind me, single file, to the other side. There, in that massive structure, we would begin learning our trades. I'd spent so many years studying, perfecting my Latin, my writing, my painting. I'd spent hours at the piano, learning Mozart and Beethoven, always with that building off in the distance—the ultimate goal.

Sophia, the valedictorian of three years ago, had stood at that same podium, reading her speech about our great responsibility as the future leaders of The New America. She spoke about becoming a doctor, and how she would work to prevent future plagues. By now she was probably saving lives in the King's capital, the City of Sand. They said he'd restored a city in the desert. I couldn't wait to get there. I wanted to be an artist, to paint portraits like Frida Kahlo or surreal dreamscapes like Magritte, frescoed across the City's great walls.

Teacher Florence rested her hand on my back. "You embody The New America, Eve—intelligence, hard work, and beauty. We're so proud of you."

The band started a much livelier song and Ruby belted out the lyrics. The girls on the lawn laughed and danced, swinging each other around and around and around until they were dizzy.

"Go on, eat some more." Headmistress Burns nudged Violet, a shorter girl with black, almond-shaped eyes, toward the food table.

"What's her problem?" Pip asked, sidling up beside me. She took the medal in her hands to get a closer look.

"You know Headmistress," I started, about to remind Pip that our head of school was seventy-five, arthritic, and had lost her entire family when the plague finally ended twelve years ago. But Pip shook her head.

"Not her—*her*."

Arden was the only twelfth year not celebrating. She leaned against the wall of the dormitory, arms crossed. Even in the unflattering gray jumper with the crest of The New American Monarchy sewn over her chest, even scowling, she was still beautiful. While most of the girls in School kept their hair long, she'd chopped her black mane into a short bob, making her fair skin look even fairer. Her hazel eyes were flecked with gold. "She's up to something, I know it," I told Pip, not taking my eyes off her. "She always is."

Pip ran her fingers over the smooth medallion. "Someone saw her swimming across the lake. . . ." she whispered.

"Swimming? I doubt that." No one in the compound could swim. We'd never been taught.

Pip shrugged. "Who knows with her." While most of the twelfth years had come to School at five years old, after the plague ended, Arden had arrived at School at eight, so there had always been something different about her. Her parents had given her over to the School until they could establish themselves in the City of Sand. She loved to remind students of the fact that, unlike the rest of us, she wasn't an orphan. When she finished learning her trade, she would retire in her parents' new apartment. She wouldn't have to work a day in her life.

Pip had decided this explained some deeper truth about Arden: because she had parents, she was not afraid to be thrown out of School. Often her rebelliousness took the form of harmless pranks—rotten figs in your oatmeal or a dead mouse on the sink, complete with a white toothpaste beehive. But other times she was mean, cruel even. Arden had cut off Ruby's long black ponytail once, just for laughing at the C she'd gotten on a Dangers of Boys and Men exam.

In the past few months, Arden had been strangely quiet, though. She was the last to meals and the first to leave, and she was always alone. I had the growing suspicion that for graduation tomorrow, she was planning her greatest prank of all.

In an instant, Arden turned and started toward the dining building, kicking up dirt as she ran. My eyes narrowed as I watched her go. I didn't need any surprises at the ceremony; I had enough to worry about with my speech. It had even been said that the King himself would be attending for the first time in the school's history. I knew it was a rumor, started by the ever-dramatic Maxine, but still. It was an important day—the most important of our lives.

"Headmistress Burns?" I asked. "May I please be excused? I left my vitamins in the dormitory." I felt around the pockets of my uniform dress, feigning frustration.

Headmistress stood beside the long table of food. "How many times do I have to remind you girls to keep them in your satchel? Go, but don't dawdle." As she spoke she stroked the snout of the roast boar, the fur on its face singed black.

"Yes," I agreed, looking over my shoulder for Arden. She had already turned the corner, past the dining hall. "I will, Headmistress." I took off running, offering Pip a quick *be right back*.

I rounded the corner, approaching the compound's main gate. Arden crouched beside the building and reached underneath a bush. She pulled her uniform dress over her head and changed into a black jumper, her milk-white skin glowing in the setting sun.

I strode toward her as she was tugging on boots—the same black leather ones the guards always wore. "Whatever you're planning, you can just forget it," I announced, pleased when she straightened up at the sound of my voice.

Arden paused a moment and then pulled the laces tight, as if she were strangling her ankles. It was a minute before she spoke and even then, she didn't turn to face me. "Please, Eve," she said quietly, "just go away."

I knelt down beside the building, holding my skirt to keep it from getting dirty. "I know you're up to something. Someone saw you by the lake." Arden moved quickly, her eyes fixed on her boots as she tied the laces in double knots. A backpack sat in a ditch beneath the bush, and she stuffed her gray uniform dress inside it. "Where'd you steal that guard's uniform from?"

She pretended she hadn't heard me, instead peering through a hole in the shrubs. I followed her gaze to the compound gate, which was opening slowly. The shipment of food for tomorrow's ceremony had just arrived on a covered green and black government Jeep. "This has nothing to do with you, Eve," she finally said.

"So what is this about then? You're impersonating a guard?" I reached for the whistle around my neck. I'd never reported Arden before, never brought anything she did to the Headmistress, but the ceremony was just too important—to me, to everyone. "I'm sorry, Arden, but I can't let you—"

Before the whistle touched my lips, Arden ripped the chain from my neck and threw it across the grass. In one swift motion, she pinned me up against the building. Her eyes were wet and bloodshot.

"You listen," she said slowly. Her forearm pressed on my neck, making it hard to breathe. "I am leaving here in exactly one minute. If you know what's good for you, you'll go back to the celebration and pretend you never saw this."

Twenty feet away, some female guards unloaded the truck, carrying boxes inside while the others pointed their machine guns toward the woods. "But there's nowhere to go. . . ." I wheezed.

"Wake up!" she hissed. "You think you're going to learn a trade?" She gestured to the brick building on the other side of the lake. I could barely see it in the growing darkness. "Don't you ever wonder why the Graduates never come outside? Or why there's a separate gate for them? Or why there are so many fences and locked doors around here? You think they're sending you there to *paint*?" At this, she finally released me.

I rubbed my neck. The skin burned where the chain had broken. "Of course," I said. "What else would we be doing?"

Arden let out a laugh as she tossed her backpack over her shoulder. Then she leaned in. I could smell the spicy boar's meat on her breath. "Ninety-eight percent of the population is dead, Eve. Gone. How do you think the world is going to continue? They don't need artists," she whispered. "They need *children*. The healthiest children they can find . . . or make."

"What are you talking about?" I asked. She picked herself up, never looking away from the truck. A guard pulled the canvas cover over the back of the Jeep and climbed into the driver's seat.

"Why do you think they're so worried about our height, our weight, what we're eating and drinking?" Arden brushed the dirt off her black jumpsuit and looked at me one last time. The area beneath her eyes was puffy, the purple veins visible under her thin white skin. "I saw them—the girls who graduated before us. And I'm not going to wind up in some hospital bed, birthing a litter every year for the next twenty years of my life."

I stumbled backward, as if she had slapped me in the face. "You're lying," I said. "You're wrong."

But Arden just shook her head. And with that she darted off toward the Jeep, pulling the black cap over her hair. She waited for the gate guards to turn before approaching. "One more!" she called out. Then she jumped onto its back bumper and pulled herself into the covered bed.

The truck bumped down the dirt road and disappeared into the dark woods. The gate closed slowly behind it. I listened to the lock click, unable to believe what I'd just seen. Arden had left School. Escaped. She had gone beyond the wall, into the wild, with nothing and no one to protect her.

I didn't believe what she'd said. I couldn't. Maybe Arden would return in a few hours, on the Jeep. Maybe this was her craziest prank yet. But as I turned back to the windowless building on the other side of the compound, I couldn't stop my hands from trembling, or the bitter vomit of jungle berries from spewing out of my mouth. I got sick there, in the dirt, a single thought consuming me: What if Arden was right?

two

AFTER WE'D BRUSHED OUR HAIR AND TEETH, WASHED our faces, and dressed in the identical white nightgowns that came down to our ankles, I lay in bed, pretending to be tired. The dormitory was buzzing with the news of Arden's disappearance. Girls poked their heads into each room to deliver the latest gossip: a barrette found in the bushes, Headmistress questioning a guard near the gate. Through it all, I wanted one of the hardest things to find at School, something so strange it was impossible to even request.

I wanted to be alone.

"Noelle thinks Arden's hiding out in the doctor's

quarters," Ruby told Pip. She surveyed the cards in her hand. "Go fish." They were sitting on Pip's narrow twin bed, playing a game they'd checked out of the School library. The old *Finding Nemo* cards were faded and ripped, some stuck together with dried fig juice.

"I bet she's just trying to get out of the ceremony," Pip added. The freckled skin on her face was dotted with dried toothpaste, which she called her "miracle blemish remover." She kept glancing at me, expecting me to speculate about Arden's whereabouts or comment on the packs of guards outside who were searching the grounds with flashlights. I didn't say a word.

I thought about what Arden had said. In the last months, Headmistress Burns had become increasingly concerned with our diets, making sure we were eating enough. She appeared at our weekly blood tests and weigh-ins and saw that we were all taking our vitamins. She'd even sent Ruby to Dr. Hertz when she got her period a week later than everyone else at School.

I pulled the thin white blanket up to my neck. Ever since I was small, I had been told there was a plan for me—a plan for all of us. Complete twelve years at School, then move across the compound and learn a trade for four years. Then onto the City of Sand, where life and freedom awaited us. We would work and live there, under the rule of the King. I had always listened to the Teachers, had no reason not to. Even now, Arden's theory made no sense. Why would we be taught to fear men when we'd ultimately have children and families of our own? Why would we be educated if we were only going to breed? The emphasis they'd put on our studies, the way we were encouraged to pursue—

"Eve? Did you hear what I said?" Pip interrupted my thoughts. She and Ruby were staring at me.

"No, what?"

Ruby gathered up the cards in her hand, her thick black hair still short and uneven from where Arden had cut it. "We want a preview of your speech before we go to bed."

My throat tightened as I thought of my final address, the three scrawled pages crumpled inside my nightstand drawer. "It's supposed to be a surprise," I said, after a moment. I had written about the power of imagination in building The New America. The words I had chosen, the future I'd described, seemed so uncertain now.

Ruby and Pip stared at me, but I turned away, unable to look them in the eye. I couldn't tell them what Arden had suggested: that the freedom of graduation was just an illusion, something created to keep us calm and content.

"Fine, suit yourself." Pip blew out the candle on her night table. I blinked a few times, adjusting my eyes to the dark. Slowly, her round face became visible in the gray moonlight streaming in from the window. "But we *are* your best friends."

Within minutes, Ruby's faint snoring filled the room. She always fell asleep first. Pip stared at the ceiling, her hands resting over her heart. "I can't wait to graduate. We're going to be learning things—real things. And in a few years we'll be out in the world, in the new city beyond the forest. It's going to be amazing, Eve. We'll be like . . . *real* people." She turned to me and I hoped, in the dim moonlight, she couldn't see the tears gathering in the corners of my eyes.

I wondered about the life that Pip and I would really have. Pip wanted to be an architect, like Frank Lloyd Wright. She wanted to build new houses that wouldn't deteriorate without human care, houses that had shelters stocked with canned edibles, where even the most microscopic of deadly viruses could not get in. I'd told her that when we finished learning our trades we'd live together in the City of Sand. We'd get an apartment like we'd read about in books, with queen-sized beds and windows where we could look out to the other side of the City, where the men lived, far away from us. We'd learn to ski on the massive indoor slopes Teacher Etta had told us about, or use our manners in the restaurants with crisp, white tablecloths and polished silverware. We'd order our dinners from a menu, asking for our meat to be cooked just the way we pleased.

"I know," I choked out. "It'll be great."

I dabbed at my eyes, thankful when Pip's breaths finally slowed. But then the guilt came, and the growing fear that tomorrow, I might not just be giving some deluded, wistful speech. I might be leading my friends to their demise.

———

I WAITED FOR SLEEP BUT IT NEVER CAME. AT THREE o'clock, I knew I could not lie there any longer. I got up and went to the window, looking across the compound. It was empty save for a lone guard, identifiable by her slight limp, canvassing the lawn in a routine sweep.

Our room was only two stories above ground. Once the guard was out of sight, I opened the window as I always did on warm nights. Then I perched on the ledge. Every year the School ran drills: what to do in a raid, what to do in an earthquake, what to do when confronted by a dog pack, what to do in a fire. Now, recalling the simple, worn diagrams Headmistress Burns had passed around at the end of class, I lowered myself outside the building and hung from the window ledge, preparing myself for the fall.

I let go and hit the ground hard. Pain shot through my ankle, but I pushed myself up from the dirt and ran as fast as I could toward the lake. Across the glittering water, the brick trade building was a black rectangle against the deep purple sky.

As I stood before the lake, its gentle waves lapping at my toes, my courage drained. We'd never learned to swim. The teachers often told stories of the days before the plague, and how people had drowned in ocean waves, or been fooled by the deceptive calm of their own man-made pools.

I glanced back at the open dorm window. In another minute the guard would round the corner with her flashlight and catch me out after dark. She'd already discovered me in the bushes after Arden had gone missing, vomit covering my dress. I had explained that I was just nervous about graduating, but I couldn't give her any more reason to be suspicious.

I waded in. Thornbushes lined the narrow shore, reaching over the water's surface. I took off my socks and wrapped them around my palms so I could grab the sharp branches. Slowly I pulled myself across, the lake water rising to my neck. I was only a yard in when the soft ground suddenly dropped out beneath my feet. Water rushed into my mouth and I squeezed the branches tighter, the thorns piercing my skin through the socks. I couldn't stifle my cough.

The guard paused on the lawn. The flashlight beam stretched across the grass and danced over the surface of the lake. I held my breath, my lungs aching from the pain. Finally the bright white beam returned to the grass and she disappeared once more around the other side of the compound.

It went on like that for over an hour. I struggled across, stopping whenever the guard limped past, careful not to make a sound. When I finally reached the other side I heaved myself up into the muddy grass. The socks around my palms were soaked through with blood and my cold, wet gown clung to my body. I peeled it off, sitting beneath the monstrous building while I wrung the water out of it.

This side of the compound was strangely empty, except for the long wooden bridge that lay across the grass, ready for the following day's ceremony. Unlike School, there were no flowers surrounding the brick structure. We were told that the Graduates were too busy to come out of the building, that their schedule was even more rigorous than the schedule at School, and what time was not spent eating, sleeping, or in class, was used for the perfection of the trade. Twelfth-year students whispered and worried about the sudden loss of the sun, but that kind of dedication had always sounded exhilarating to me.

The tall grass came up around my body, but it was not enough cover. I pulled my damp gown back over my head and ran around to the corner of the building. It *did* have windows, about five feet off the ground, just not on the side facing School.

Hope bloomed inside me, a lightness that made each movement easier. I found a rusty spigot along the wall, with a bucket beside it. I turned the bucket over, using it as a stepstool, and hoisted myself up to get a better look. Inside was my future, and as I reached for the window ledge I wanted it to be the one I had imagined, not the one Arden was running from. I prayed I'd see a room filled with girls in their beds, the walls decorated with oil paintings of wild dogs sprinting across the plains. I prayed for drafting tables covered in blueprints and books piled high on each nightstand. I prayed that I was not wrong, that tomorrow I would graduate and the future I had imagined would open up before me like a morning glory in the sun.

My hands clung to the ledge as I pulled myself closer. I pressed my nose against the window. There, on the other side of the glass, was a girl on a narrow bed, her abdomen covered with bloodied gauze. Her blond hair was matted. Her arms were strapped down with leather restraints.

Beside her was another girl, her giant stomach stretching nearly three feet over her body, the thinned skin covered with purple veins. Then the girl opened her deep green eyes and stared at me for a moment, until they rolled back in her head. It was Sophia. Sophia, who'd given her own valedictory speech three years ago, about becoming a doctor.

I covered my mouth to suppress a scream.

There were rows of girls in cots, most with massive stomachs beneath the white sheets. A few had their middles bandaged. One had scars that snaked over her side, deep pink and puffy. Across the room, another girl writhed in pain, trying to free her wrists. Her mouth was open, yelling something I couldn't hear beyond the glass.

The nurses appeared, entering from doors that lined

the long, factory-like room. Dr. Hertz followed right behind them, her wiry gray hair impossible to miss. She was the one who determined the vitamin recipes we consumed every day and met with us each month to check our health. She was the one who put us on the table and prodded us with cold instruments, never answering our questions, never meeting our gaze.

The girl's neck whipped back and forth as the doctor approached her, pressing a hand down on her forehead. The girl continued yelling, and a few sleeping patients awoke from the sound. They pulled at their restraints, cried out, the faint chorus barely audible. Then, in one swift motion, the doctor jabbed a needle into the girl's arm and she went horribly still. Dr. Hertz held it up to the others—a threat—and the shouting stopped.

I lost my grip on the window ledge and fell backward, the bucket coming out from underneath me. I curled up on the hard earth, my insides choked. It all made sense now. The injections given by Dr. Hertz—the ones that made us nauseated, irritable, and sore. Headmistress petting my hair as I took my vitamins. The empty stare Teacher Agnes gave me when I spoke of my future as a muralist.

There would be no trade, no city, no apartment with

a queen-sized bed and a window overlooking the street. No eating at the restaurants with the polished silverware and crisp, white tablecloths. There would only be that room, the putrid stink of old bedpans, skin stretched until it cracked. There would only be babies cut out of my womb, ripped from my arms and shuttled somewhere beyond these walls. I'd be left screaming, bleeding, alone, and then plunged back into a dreamless, drug-induced sleep.

I struggled to my feet and started toward the shore. The night was darker, the air colder, and the lake much wider and deeper than before. Still, I didn't look back. I had to get away from that building, that room, those girls with the dead eyes.

I had to get away.

three

WHEN I GOT BACK TO SCHOOL I WAS SOAKING WET, WITH blood dripping from my hands. I hadn't even bothered to wrap my socks around my palms as I crossed the lake, I was so focused on simply putting distance between myself and that building. I had let the thorns dig into my skin, my eyes locked on my bedroom window, numb to the pain.

As the guard circled the back of the dormitories I ran up the shore, my nightgown heavy with water. A few torches were still lit, but the lawn was dark, and I could hear the owls in the trees, like great cheerleaders, urging me on. Before that night I had never broken a rule. I was seated before every class started, my books open on my desk. I studied two extra hours every evening. I even cut my food carefully, as instructed, my pointer finger pressing on the back of the knife. But only one rule mattered now. *Never go beyond the wall*, Teacher Agnes had said, in the Dangers of Boys and Men seminar when she'd explained the act of rape. She'd stared at us with her watery, red-rimmed eyes until we repeated it back to her, our voices a coaxed monotone.

Never go beyond the wall.

But no gang of men or hungry wolf den beyond the wall could be worse than the fate I faced locked within it. In the wild there would be choice—however dangerous, however frightening. I would decide what I wanted to eat, where I wanted to go. The sun would still warm my skin.

Maybe I could get out the gate, like Arden had. Wait until morning, when the last shipment of supplies came in for the celebration. A window would be harder. The one by the library was close to the wall, but it was a fifty-foot drop and I would need rope, a plan, some way to lower myself down.

Inside, I crept toward the narrow, dimly lit staircase, careful not to make a sound. It would be impossible for me to save everyone. But I had to get to my bedroom and wake Pip. Maybe we could bring Ruby, too. There wouldn't be much time to explain, but we'd pack a bag with some clothes and figs and the gold-wrapped candies Pip loved. We'd leave tonight, forever. There would be no looking back.

I bounded up to the second floor and down the hall, past room after room of girls tucked neatly into their beds. Through a doorway I could see Violet curled up, smiling in her sleep, oblivious to what awaited her the next day. I was steps from my bedroom when the hallway glowed with an eerie light.

"Who's there?" a gravelly voice asked.

I turned slowly, the blood cooling in my veins. Teacher Florence stood at the end of the hall, holding a kerosene lantern. It threw black, looming shadows on the wall behind her.

"I was only . . ." I trailed off. The lake water was dripping from the hem of my skirt, forming a puddle around my feet.

Teacher Florence came toward me, her sun-spotted face grimacing in displeasure. "You went across the lake," she said. "You saw the Graduates."

I nodded, thinking again of Sophia in her hospital bed, how her eyes retreated into the blue-ringed hollows of her face. The bruising on her wrists and ankles, where she pulled against the leather straps. The pressure was building inside me, like a kettle just before the boil. I wanted to scream. To jolt everyone upright in bed. To grab this frail woman by the shoulders and bury my fingers into her arms until she understood the pain that I understood then, the panic and confusion. The betrayal.

But all those years of quietly sitting, my hands folded neatly in my lap, of listening and speaking only when spoken to, kept me in practiced obedience. What if I yelled now, into the silent night? There was nothing I could say that would convince the other girls. They would never believe the trades were a lie. They'd think I'd gone mad. Eve, the girl who broke under the stress of graduation. Eve, the lunatic who ranted about pregnant Graduates. *Pregnant Graduates!* They'd laugh. I'd be sent to that building a day earlier than everyone else, forced into permanent silence.

"I'm sorry," I offered, "I was just . . ." The tears slipped from my eyes.

Teacher Florence took the palm of my hand in hers, tracing the creases where blood had pooled and dried. "I can't let you leave the compound like this." Her stiff white hair grazed my chin as she examined the punctured skin.

"I know, I'm sorry. I'll go back to bed and—"

"No," she said calmly. When she looked up her eyes were glassy. "Like *this*." She pulled a handkerchief from the pocket of her nightgown and wrapped it around my hand. "I can help you, but we'll need to clean you up. Quickly. If Headmistress finds out, she'll punish us both. Go get your things and meet me downstairs."

I would've hugged her then, but she nudged me toward my door. I was taking off into my bedroom, preparing to get Pip and Ruby, when Teacher called after me, her voice still a whisper.

"Eve, you'll go alone—you mustn't disturb anyone else." I started to protest, but she was firm. "It's the only way," she said solemnly, and then she was halfway down the corridor, the lantern swinging in her hand.

I moved around my room in the dark, noiselessly packing up the only knapsack I owned. Pip lay motionless in the bed. *You'll go alone,* Teacher's directive rang in my ears. But I'd spent a lifetime doing what I was told, only to be deceived. I could wake Pip and beg Teacher to help us both. But what if Pip didn't believe me? What if she woke the others? And what if Teacher said she couldn't help both of us, that two of us would never make it out together unnoticed? Then it would be over for us both. Forever.

Pip rolled over and mumbled something in her sleep. I took the pair of pants I had from our exercises, and the silk pouch of my favorite things. It contained a tiny plastic bird I'd found years ago while digging in the mud. A gold wrapper from the first sucking candy Headmistress had ever given me; the small, tarnished silver bracelet saved from when I'd arrived at school at five; and finally the only letter I had from my mother, the paper yellow and tearing at every crease.

I zipped up the bag, wishing I had more time. Pip's pale face was pressed against her pillow, her lips puttering with her breath. I had read once, in one of those pre-plague books in the library, that love was bearing witness. That it was the act of watching someone's life, of simply being there to say: *your life is worth seeing.* If that is true then I have never loved anyone as much as I loved Pip, and no one has ever loved me that much either. For Pip was there when I twisted my wrist doing handstands on the lawn. She was the one who held me after I lost my favorite blue pin, which I was told belonged to my mother. And she was the one who sang with me in the shower, to the songs we'd discovered on the old records in the archives. *Let it be, let it be!* Pip would belt, with shampoo suds running down her face and a voice that was always a little out of tune. *Whisper words of wisdom, let it beeeee.*

I headed for the door, glancing at her one last time. Pip had heard me crying that first night at School and laid down in the bed beside me and let me bury my face in her neck. She'd waved to the ceiling and told me, in heaven, our mothers were watching. From heaven they loved us.

"I'll come back for you," I said. I nearly choked on the words. "I will," I said again.

If I didn't go then, though, I never would, so I ran through the hall, down the staircase and toward the doctor's office, where I found Teacher waiting for me with a sack full of food.

She pulled the thorns from my palms with tweezers. Then she bandaged my hands, her eyes on the gauze as she wrapped it around, layer upon layer. It was a while before she spoke.

"It began with fertility doctors," Teacher said. "The King believed the science was the key to repopulating the earth quickly, efficiently, without all the complications of families, marriage, and love. He thought if you were given an education, you would be occupied and content. He thought that if you feared men, you girls would breed willingly without them. And when the first Graduates went into that building, some of them did. But the process is extreme. And there are often complications with multiple births. In these last few years it's gotten worse, and I'm worried it will get even worse still."

I glanced again at the drawer where Dr. Hertz kept our weekly shots, the ones that made our breasts sore and had girls doubled over with cramps. The counter was covered in glass jars of vitamins, which were organized in our pill-boxes according to the days. We swallowed them down morning, afternoon, and night, like colorful, sugarcoated poisons.

"So you've always known then—about the Graduates?" I asked.

Teacher peered out the blinds. When she was sure the guard had passed, she gestured for me to follow her out the back door and into the night. Feral dogs howled in the distance, a sound that sent my heart racing. We walked along the perimeter of the wall. Teacher turned around, making sure we were far enough in front of the guard that we wouldn't be seen. When she spoke again, her voice was much lower than before.

"The plague came first," she began, "and then the vaccine made it much worse. The world was consumed by death, Eve. There was no order; people were confused. Scared. The King took over and then you had to make a choice. Follow him or be in the wild alone."

She didn't look at me as she spoke, but I could see the tears brimming in her eyes. I thought of the annual speeches, how we'd crowd together in the dining hall and listen to the single radio set on the table in front of Headmistress. The King, Our Great Leader, The Only Man to be Respected, would call to us from those old speakers. He'd tell us of the progress made in the City of Sand, of the skyscrapers that were being built, of the wall that could keep armies, viruses, and the threats of the wilderness out. He said The New America started there, that there would only be one chance to rebuild. He said we would be safe.

"I was already fifty," Teacher continued. "My family had died. I had no choice. I couldn't survive on my own. But you have the chance I didn't."

We came to the apple tree that stretched its boughs in front of the wall. Pip and I had sat beneath it a hundred times before, eating its fruit and feeding the rotten apples to the squirrels. "Where will I go?" I asked, my voice trembling.

"If you continue straight for two miles you'll come to a road." Her thin lips moved slowly as she spoke, the skin flaky and chapped. "It will be dangerous. Find the signs marked eighty and go west, toward the setting sun. Stay near the road but not on it."

"And then what?" I asked. She reached into the pocket of her nightgown and pulled out a key, cradling it in her wrinkled hands like a jewel.

"If you keep going you'll reach the ocean. On the other side of the red bridge there's a camp. I've heard it called *Califia*. If you can get there, they'll protect you."

"And what about the City of Sand?" I asked as she felt along the wall. The conversation was ending, I could sense it, and questions flooded my mind. "What about the babies that are being born? Who's going to take care of them? And the Graduates, will they ever get out?"

"The babies are taken to the city. The Graduates . . ." She kept her head down, feeling along the wall. "They are in the service of the King. They'll get out if and when the King decides it is time, if and when enough children have been produced."

Behind some branches was a hole so small it was barely noticeable. Teacher Florence inserted the key and in one turn the wall opened out, the doorway finally visible. Then she glanced backward, to the other side of the compound.

"It's supposed to be an emergency fire exit," she explained.

The forest spilled out before me, its hillsides lit only by the perfect, glowing moon. This was it. Where I came from, where I was going. My past, my future. I wanted to ask Teacher more—about this strange place called Califia, about the danger of the road—but just then the beam of the guard's flashlight rounded the corner of the dormitory building.

Teacher Florence pushed me forward. "Go, now!" she urged. "Go!"

And as fast as the door opened, it closed behind me, leaving me alone in the cold, starless night.

four

THE FIRST THING I SAW WHEN I OPENED MY EYES WAS the sky: a blue, boundless thing that was so much bigger than I had ever imagined. All twelve years I had been at School I had seen only the stretch between one side of the wall and the other. Now I stood underneath it, noticing the purple and yellow streaks that appeared in that massive umbrella, visible now in the early morning light.

Last night I had run as far and as fast as I could, too terrified to stop. I went under crumbling bridges and through steep ravines, until I saw that beautiful sign *80* lit up by the moon. It was then that I found rest in a ditch, my legs simply too tired to carry me any farther. The bottom of my pants was caked with dirt and my throat was dry.

I climbed up onto a hard, flat ridge and looked out on the morning. The hillside was covered with overgrown flower bushes, tall, terrifically green grass, and trees that sprouted up at unusual angles, winding in and out and around one another. I couldn't help but laugh, remembering the pictures I had seen of the world before the plague. There were photos of neat, manicured lawns, and rows of houses on paved streets, their bushes trimmed into perfect squares. This looked nothing like that at all.

On the horizon, a deer bounded through an old gas station. Before the plague, oil had powered nearly everything. But without anyone to run the refineries, they had closed down. Now oil was used only by the King's government, including a set allowance for each School. The deer stopped to feast on the grass that had sprung up between the rusted pumps. Dense flocks of birds changed directions in the sky, their wings iridescent in the bright morning light. I stomped on the ground, feeling the ledge beneath me, so hard and flat. The road was an inch thick with moss.

"Hello?" a voice asked. "Hello?"

I spun around, looking for the source, my fear returning

at the sound of a man's voice. I remembered the tales of the forest and the renegade gangs who camped out there, living in the trees. My eyes fell on a weathered shack a few yards off. It was covered in ivy, the door sealed shut. I crept toward it, trying to hide myself.

The voice spoke again. "Shut up!"

I froze. We weren't allowed to speak those words at School. They were "inappropriate" and only known to us through books.

"Shut up!" The voice yelled again, from somewhere above me.

I turned my face skyward. There, a large red parrot perched on the roof of the shack, its head cocked to one side as he studied me.

"Ring, ring! Ring, ring! Who is this?" He pecked at something on the roof.

I had seen a parrot in a children's book before, about a pirate who robbed people of treasure. Pip and I had read it in the archives, running our fingers over the water-stained illustrations.

Pip. Somewhere miles away, she was discovering my empty bed, the sheets crumpled and cold. New plans for graduation would be made in haste. She and Ruby were probably afraid that I had been kidnapped, unable to imagine I would ever leave of my own volition. Maybe Amelia, the all-too-eager salutatorian, would give my speech and lead them over the bridge. When would they realize the truth? When they set foot on the bare bank on the other side? When the doors flung open, exposing the cement room?

I reached for the bird, but it backed away. "What's your name?" I asked. My voice startled me.

The bird stared at me with its black beady eyes. "Peter! Where are you Peter?" it said, hopping along the roof.

"Was Peter your owner?" I asked. The parrot preened itself with its claw. "Where did you come from?" I imagined Peter had long since died in the plague, or abandoned the bird in the chaos afterward. The parrot had survived, though, for over a decade. That simple fact filled me with hope.

I wanted to ask the bird more questions, but then it flew off, until it was only a speck of red against the blue sky. I followed its path, watching it disappear in the distance. Then my gaze fell on the silhouettes coming toward the road, over the hillside and through the trees. Even from two hundred feet away, I could see the guns slung over their backs.

For a moment I stood in awe of these strange and unfamiliar creatures. They were so much taller and broader than women. Even their gait was different, heavier, as though it required great effort to take even one step. They all wore pants and boots and some were shirtless, revealing their leathery brown chests.

The figures moved as a pack, until one brought up his gun and aimed for the deer grazing near the gas pumps. With one blast it fell, its leg seizing in pain. Only then did the panic set in. I was in the middle of the wild, in unforgiving daylight. A gang was just thirty yards off. I fumbled with the door of the shack, clawing at the ivy until I found the rusty old lock.

The gang came closer. I kept at the lock, pulling and hitting it with my palm, hoping it would break. *Please open*, I begged, *please*. I glanced around the corner of the shack again and saw the men beneath the gas station awning. They huddled around the deer. One hacked at the animal, cutting its coat away like a person skinning fruit. It bucked and twisted. It was still alive.

I tugged on the door, suddenly wishing Headmistress would barrel down the broken road and the guards would pull me onto the bed of a government Jeep. We would go back the way I'd come, the men shooting at us, until they were tiny black dots on the horizon. Until I was safe.

But my fantasy evaporated, like fog burned off by the sun. Headmistress wasn't my protector, and School was no longer safe.

Nowhere was safe.

The lock finally gave and I fell forward into the dark shack. I pulled my knapsack inside and shut the door, pushing farther down a narrow corridor that emptied out into a larger room. The dirt-caked windows were snaked with vines, making it impossible to see. I felt my way in and realized at once that it wasn't a shack, but a long house that expanded into the side of the hill, half buried by the grass. I kept going, feeling my way farther into the room. The walls were rough and mottled, as though they were made of stones.

The strange voices came closer. "Come on, Raff, just throw the hide in the bag and let's get off."

"Shove it, you filthy crumb," another shot back. Their voices were deep and gruff. They didn't speak in the same careful English we'd learned in School.

I had sat in my Dangers of Boys and Men class for an entire year, learning all the ways women were vulnerable to the other sex. First was the Manipulation and Heartache unit. We did a close reading of *Romeo and Juliet*, studying the way Romeo seduced Juliet and ultimately led her to her death. Teacher Mildred gave a lecture about a relationship she had before the plague and the highs that so quickly evolved into desperate, anger-fueled lows. She cried as she described how her "love" had left her after she gave birth to their first child, a little girl who later died in the plague. He'd claimed something called "confusion." During the unit on Domestic Enslavement, we saw old print ads of women in aprons. But the lesson on Gang Mentality was the most terrifying of all.

Teacher Agnes showed us secret images taken by security cameras perched on the wall. They were blurry, but there were three figures—three men. They cornered another, stole the supplies at his belt, and executed him with a shotgun. For weeks I woke up in the middle of the night, my skin slick with sweat. I kept seeing that white blast and the man's limp body splayed out on the ground, his legs twisted.

"You didn't need another one, you kill-happy Buggum!" another voice yelled. I backed farther into the house, pressing up against a rough, unstable wall. The air was hot and thick with the scent of mold and something sharper, something chemical. I pulled my shirt over my face, trying to muffle my breath as the men stomped past.

They were close now. I could hear them, each step cracking fallen branches with vicious snaps and pops. Someone stopped outside the shack. His breaths were raspy and choked with phlegm. "Whatcha gots there?" another one called. His voice was farther off, higher. Maybe on the road.

He cleared his throat and terror filled my chest. I held onto the wall of stones, trying to steady myself as I closed my eyes. Go *away, please, please,* I thought.

"Lock's broken! Go on ahead, gonna take a looky here."

I pushed back as far as I could, wishing the cold stones would give way, that I could sink into them, disappear behind their pitted surface. There had been so many lessons on what was beyond the wall. Teacher Helene had held up the photographs of the woman who had had half her face mauled off by a rabid dog. But they'd only ever suggested one thing if we found ourselves outside, in the wild. They hadn't taught us survival skills. I couldn't make a fire, I couldn't hunt, and I wouldn't be able to fight this man off. *Get back in*, Teacher had said simply. *Do whatever it takes to get back to School.*

The door swung open. I was ready for him to plow forward, to drag me, screaming, outside. But as light flooded the long shack, I no longer cared about the gang on the road or the images from class or the intentions of the man standing around the corner, just twenty feet away. For the sunlight revealed walls made not of rough stones, but of hundreds of skulls, the black, hollow eye cavities peering back at me. I covered my mouth to keep from screaming.

"Just a morgue," the man yelled. And then the door closed behind him, leaving me in the dark with the skeletons. I stayed there, shaking, for hours, until I was certain the men were gone.

BY THE EIGHTH DAY MY LEGS ACHED AND MY THROAT burned. I moved slowly through thick brush on the side of the road, knocking back the branches with a broken tree limb I'd been using as a walking stick. I kept telling myself I would get to Califia. I kept telling myself that I would be safe soon, that as long as I stayed in the overgrowth, out of sight, the gangs wouldn't find me. But my water bottle had been sucked dry days ago. Fatigue was chasing me. One moment I was sweating and the next I was shivering from the cold.

I'd moved west like Teacher Florence had instructed, toward the setting sun. At night, when the temperature dropped, I slept in the closets of abandoned houses or in garages, beside the shells of old cars. When I found a place I thought was safe I'd sit for a while, eating the apples Teacher had packed for me and thinking about School. I kept turning over that night in my head, wondering if it could have been different—if I could've saved Pip too. Maybe I should've taken the chance. Maybe I should've woken her up. Maybe I should've at least tried. My chest heaved with sobs when I imagined her strapped to one of those beds, alone and afraid, wondering why I'd left her.

It wasn't long before I ran out of food. The cabinets of the homes were bare, scavenged by survivors in the aftermath of the plague. I tried to pick berries, but a few handfuls were not enough to appease the burning in my stomach. I grew weaker, my steps slower, until it was hard to walk more than a mile without having to stop for rest. I would sit at the base of trees, their gnarled roots holding me, and watch the deer bound through the tall grass.

Sometimes, right before the sun went down, I'd take my things out of my knapsack to look at them. I kept returning to that bracelet, so small it could barely fit around three of my fingers.

Like all the girls at School, I'd been an orphan. I'd come when I was five years old, after my mother was taken by the plague. I had never known my father. These items were the only things left from my past, with the exception of a few memories—feelings, really—of a mother combing the knots out of my wet hair, or the smell of her perfume as she rocked me to bed. I'd read once about amputees, and how they had pains where their arms or legs used to be. Phantom limbs, they were called. I'd always thought that was the best way to describe my feelings about my mother. She was now just an ache for something I'd had and lost.

I continued on, putting more and more of my weight on my walking stick. In the distance I spotted a tiny plastic pool where rainwater had collected, a bright turquoise oasis surrounded by weeds. I blinked twice, wondering if I was hallucinating from the day's heat. I ran to it and fell, my lips touching the cool water. I wondered how long it had been there, if it was clean enough to consume, but it felt so good in my dry mouth that I didn't stop until my stomach was painfully full. When I sat back I noticed a reflection on the surface of the water. There, a few yards off, was a house, lit from within.

I started toward the glowing light as the sun kissed the treetops. I didn't know who was there or if they could help me, but I needed to at least find out.

A wooden playground had nearly collapsed in the yard.

Vines wound around the swing's rusted chain, yanking it toward the earth. Maneuvering under the broken slide, I approached a half-open window and peered inside. The living room was small, with only a rotted couch and a few cracked photographs hanging on the wall. A hooded figure crouched over a fire, cooking.

The smoke billowed up to the ceiling and spread outward, teasing my nostrils with the promise of a meat dinner. The figure picked at a leg of rabbit, feverishly biting at the bone. My mouth filled with spit just imagining how delicious it would taste.

I had seen a Stray before, grazing past the wall, in the section visible from the library's corner window. Strays were not part of gangs, not part of the King's regime, but outsiders who lived in the wild. We had been told Strays were dangerous, but this one had the slight build of a woman, which eased my fear.

"Hello there!" I called through the window. "I need help. Please!"

The figure sprung up from the floor and backed against the wall, holding the knife aloft.

"Show yourself!" Her hood was so large it shielded her face, but her dainty lips, greasy from the meat, were visible in the firelight.

"All right, please," I said, raising my hands in front of me. I pushed at the window and the rusty hinges broke off, nearly sending it crashing into the room. I pulled myself inside, keeping my hands where she could see them. "I've run out of food."

She kept her knife outstretched in my direction. She had on dark green fatigues like the ones the government workers wore and her black hooded shirt was much too big. I couldn't see her eyes.

Then, as I lowered my hands to my sides I saw the opened knapsack with the School uniform inside. The crest of The New America shone red and blue. I stepped back, slowly taking in her black combat boots, her tall frame, the beauty mark above her lip. *"Arden?"*

She pulled back her hood. Her short black hair was caked with dirt and her pale skin was sunburned, the ridge of her nose peeling in places.

I threw my arms around her, clinging tight as though she were the only thing keeping me from falling off the earth. I breathed in, not minding that we both smelled of sweat-soaked clothes.

Arden was here. Alive. With me.

"What the hell do you think you're doing?" she asked, pushing me off. "How did you get here?" Her face seized in anger and I remembered, suddenly, that she hated me.

I sat down on the floor of the room, stunned. "I escaped. You were right—I saw them, too. The girls? In that cement room?" Arden paced in front of the fire, her knife clutched in her hand. "I followed the sign that said eighty . . ." I trailed off, realizing she must've done the same.

"Califia can't be more than a week away, we'll find the red bridge soon—"

Arden tapped the flat end of the knife against her leg as she paced. "You can't stay with me. I can't let you, I'm sorry but you'll just have to—"

"No." I thought only of the giant rats that scurried over my legs at night, my poor attempt at hunting rabbits. "You can't, Arden. You wouldn't throw me out."

Arden dragged the knife along the brick fireplace and it made a scraping sound that stiffened my spine. "This is not a game, Eve. This is not some little vacation you're taking from school." She pointed out the window. "There are men and dogs and all sorts of wild animals out there, and they all want to kill us. You're not going to be able to keep up. I—I can't risk it. We'd be better on our own."

I sat on my shaking hands, my palms digging into the moldy carpet, sobered by Arden's cruelty. Even if I had found a second year in the jungle and her leg was broken in half I wouldn't have left her there—I couldn't have. It was a death sentence.

"I know it's not a game. That's why we should stick together." I needed Arden, but I couldn't quite reason why *she* needed *me*. I searched my mind anyway, trying to appeal to that cold, Darwinian part of her. "I can help you."

Arden sank onto the old couch, its cushion broken in places by twisted, rusty springs. "And how is that?" She pulled a dead beetle from the tangled ends of her hair and flicked it into the fire. It let out a loud pop.

"I'm smart. I can help with maps and compasses. And it'll help to have an extra person, to serve as lookout."

Arden let out all the air in her lungs. "There are no maps and compasses, Eve. And you're *book* smart," she corrected, holding up her finger. "That doesn't mean anything here. Can you fish? Can you hunt? Would you kill someone if it was me against them?"

I swallowed hard, knowing the answer: *no*. Of course not. I'd never even killed a slug. I'd told Teacher about the girls who salted them just to watch them squirm. But I wanted to prove to Arden that every one of those years I'd spent in the library and she'd been playing horseshoes on the lawn had been worthwhile. "Headmistress gave me the Medal of Achievement. . . ."

Arden threw her head back and laughed. "You *are* funny. But I've been fine on my own. You, however . . ."

I looked down, seeing myself through her eyes. My School jumper had been torn by a tree branch. My palms were crusted with blood and my arms were bare even though it was a cold spring night. I felt weak—weaker than I'd ever been at School, with no food and no water and no sustenance to look forward to. My eyes filled with tears.

"You don't understand—you have parents, somewhere to go. You don't know what it's like to be out here alone."

I put my face in my hands and cried. I didn't want to rot, alone, in the woods. I didn't want to starve or be captured by a man. I didn't want to *die*.

It was a good minute before I noticed Arden had moved from her post on the couch and set another piece of rabbit's meat on the fire. "You don't have to be such a baby about it," she said, passing me the stick. I devoured it, letting the juices drip down my hands and run over my chin, at once forgetting my manners.

"I can't waste any more time. My parents might have heard by now that I left School . . . they might be searching for me," Arden said when I was finally finished.

I felt the urge to roll my eyes, but stopped myself. Even now, lost in the wild, Arden was bragging about her parents. Soon she'd be telling me about the four-story house they'd lived in together, how she'd slept on a king-sized bed, even as a child. How hard it was for her to say good-bye to all of it, if only for a number of years. She missed the maids, the dinners served on china, the parents who took her to plays, letting her rest her chin on the balcony's railing to get a better view of the stage.

"You can stay tonight. Then we'll see," Arden said. She tossed me a tattered gray blanket.

I wrapped the blanket around my shoulders as the fire dwindled down to a pile of smoldering ash. "Thank you."

"No problem." Arden turned over in her pile of quilts, which were arranged on the couch, circling her like a giant bird's nest. "I found it on some skeleton a few miles back." She let out a low laugh.

I threw it off my shoulders and rested my back in the corner. I didn't care if my teeth chattered from the cold, as they had every other night.

In the light of the crescent moon, I could see photos on the wall. A young family was posed in front of the house. They were smiling, their arms wrapped around one another, as unaware of their future as I was of my own.

THE NEXT AFTERNOON I FOLLOWED ARDEN THROUGH A field of sunflowers, pushing the giant black-eyed monsters away from my face. We'd barely spoken, except to agree on a roast rabbit breakfast, and I took that as a good sign. I was half expecting to wake up with no food, no blankets, and no Arden. But she hadn't left me, and I wondered if her silence meant we'd stick together. I hoped so, if only for my stomach's sake.

We trekked down the grassy street of an abandoned neighborhood. The roofs of the houses were caved in and a few basketball hoops lined the trail, vines transforming them into lush, flowered topiaries. We passed the wreckage of old cars, their windshields shattered and their doors rusted shut. Two rotting coffins sat in an overgrown driveway: one for an adult, and one for a child.

In my mother's last days, I played outside, alone. She'd locked me out of her bedroom, for fear I'd catch her sickness. I'd lay my doll on the stone ledge in our backyard and tend to her with potions of mashed-up leaves and mud. *You'll feel better soon*, I'd told her, as I listened to my mother's cries through the open window. *The doctor is coming*, I'd whispered. *He'll save you. He's just so busy now.*

"You're morbid, aren't you?" Arden said. She tugged on my arm. I had stopped by the wood boxes, my eyes fixed on the smaller one.

"Sorry." I kept on down the road, trying to shake my melancholy mood. I felt worse, lonelier somehow, knowing that Arden didn't understand. I picked some wildflowers, clinging to the colorful bouquet.

"I've decided we can travel to Califia together," Arden said, kicking through the tall grass. "But after that you're on your own. I'll rest there, but then I have to keep moving, to find a way to reach my parents inside the City."

"Really?" I asked, my sadness giving way to relief. "Oh, Arden, I—"

Arden spun around, her eyes squinting in the sunlight. "Don't push it. I can still change my mind. . . ."

We walked in silence for a while. My thoughts drifted back to School, to that night I'd left. To the rumors that Arden had been seen swimming across the lake. They didn't seem so implausible now, after eating the meat she'd hunted, skinned, and cooked. "Is it true that you can swim?" I finally asked.

"Where'd you hear that?" Arden stripped off her black hooded sweatshirt, exposing her pale arms. Her shoulders were dusted with freckles.

"Someone saw you." I didn't mention it had taken me an hour to get across the lake, clinging to those thorny branches.

Arden smiled, like she was remembering something funny. "I taught myself. That would never occur to you, huh, Miss Valedictorian?"

I ignored her. "You weren't afraid they'd catch you?" Up ahead, a gray rabbit hopped across the road.

"The guards usually aren't out past twelve, unless they're on some special duty. Most nights the compound is pretty quiet." Arden stalked toward the rabbit, her knife outstretched in front of her. It froze as she crept closer.

I couldn't get the image of her swimming out of my

head. I'd never seen anyone do it before. Had she ventured into the water and flailed her arms? Did she hold onto something? A tree limb, a rope? "But weren't you afraid you would drown?"

At the sound of my voice, the rabbit bounded off into the overgrown remnants of a front yard.

"Nice one, Eve," Arden huffed, as she eased the knife back into her belt. "I'd love to have a heart to heart, really, but I need to hunt for our dinner." She took off between the houses, not bothering to look back.

"I'll find my own dinner!" I called after her. "Meet you back at the cottage?"

She didn't respond. I started down the trail, following it out of the neighborhood and back toward a strip of decrepit stores. An old restaurant was covered with tall grass, a giant yellow *M* just visible through vines and moss. A massive building sat at the end of the block. Its facade was still sturdy but letters had fallen off the sign. It read: WAL MA T. Scrawled in spray paint across the broken front windows were the words: QUARANTINE AREA. ENTER AT YOUR OWN RISK.

When the truck came through the barricades to evacuate any healthy children who were left, my mother begged them to take me. I flung myself on the mailbox, my thin arms wrapped around its wooden post, desperate to stay. It was useless. She appeared in the doorway as they put me on the truck's bed, blood running from her nose. Her eyes were sunken in, the color of rotting plums. Her sternum jutted from her chest like a sacrificial necklace. She stood there and waved good-bye. Blew me a kiss.

Now, moving through the abandoned town, I tried not to look at the giant wooden crosses in the parking lot, or the piles of bones beneath them, enveloped in moss. But everywhere I turned there were signs of death. Across the street the windows of an abandoned shop called Northern California Real Estate were boarded up. Coffins were stacked inside a place called Suzy's Nails. I was staring at the red X painted on the side of a Dumpster when something moved in front of me. A bear cub sauntered across the trail and gazed at me. Then he turned his attention back to a rusty can of food, which he tried to pry open with his paws.

I thought of *Winnie the Pooh*, the archived book Teacher Florence would read to us when we were children, about the bear and his good friend Christopher Robin. She had warned us that most bears were not so friendly, but this baby cub seemed too tiny to be dangerous. I wondered if he was craving honey, or if that was just some strange fiction from the story.

I reached out, careful not to startle him. The bear sniffed my arm with its wet nose. I petted the little thing's soft, brown coat, enjoying the way it scratched lightly at my skin.

"Yes, you are just like Winnie," I said. He started off toward the side of the trail to sniff at some more old cans. I wondered if Arden would let me bring him back to the house. Maybe we could keep him there for a while. I'd never had a pet before.

I reached for him again, but pulled my hand back when I heard a deafening growl. A massive bear stood on her hind legs just off the road. She towered above me.

The cub padded over to her and she opened her mouth again, showing her teeth. I straightened up, the hair on the back of my neck bristling in fear. Tremors shook my hands. The bear charged forward, her head down, and my thin arms came up in a pathetic block. I braced myself for her attack when something struck her in the face.

A rock. As the bear growled again, another stone struck her head, and she fell back, her massive bottom meeting the road. I turned around. A filthy, dirt-caked boy sat atop a black horse, clutching a slingshot in his hand. His skin was tanned a reddish brown and his muscular chest was speckled with mud.

"You better climb on," he said, tucking the slingshot in the back pocket of his pants. "This isn't over."

I glanced back at the bear, who was shaking her head, momentarily stunned. I didn't know which was worse: to be killed by some brute animal or be taken off with a wild Neanderthal on horseback. The boy reached out his hand. His fingernails were crusted with black.

"Come on!" he urged.

I took his hand in my own and he pulled me up behind him, onto the horse's bare rump. He smelled of sweat and smoke.

With one *hiyah!* we took off down the moss-covered road. I kept a hand around his chest and turned to look at the bear. She was up, running after us, her giant brown body heaving with the effort.

The boy held onto the cracked leather reins, steering the horse off the main strip and into a wide field. The bear was so close she snapped at the horse's tail.

"Faster! You have to go faster!" I cried.

The horse picked up its pace, but the bear was still too close, with no sign of tiring. I could feel my legs, slick with sweat, slipping. I clung to the boy, my fingernails digging into his skin. He leaned forward and the wind whipped over us. The bear snapped its vicious jaws again.

I looked over the boy's shoulder and saw a ravine ahead. It was nearly five feet across, and looked like an old sewage canal, fifteen feet deep. "Watch out!" I cried, but the boy kept on, even faster than before.

"Why don't you let me do the driving?" he yelled over his shoulder. Behind us, the bear ran at full speed, her dark eyes locked on the horse's rear.

"Don't," I said softly as we sped toward the ravine. If we didn't make it, the bear would surely maul us alive. We'd be trapped at the bottom of the canal with no place to hide. "Please, don't." But the horse was already lifting off, its front legs stretching toward the other side of the cliff.

My stomach rose and fell. For one moment I was weightless, and then there was the hard impact of hooves on ground. I looked out onto the field of marigolds around us. We had made it across.

I turned back one last time, afraid the bear would be upon us, but she'd slipped at the ledge. The last thing I heard was her angry roar as she skidded down the gravelly cliff and landed, hard, in the ravine's muddy pit.

seven

IT WAS A LONG WHILE BEFORE EITHER OF US SPOKE.
Now, out of danger, I pushed back on the rear of the
horse, trying to get as far away from the boy as possible.
He was a strange breed of man, part wild. Not the sophis-
ticated kind who graced the pages of *The Great Gatsby*.
Nor did he seem like the violent men I'd encountered on
my first day in the wild. He had saved me, at least. I could
only hope it wasn't for some nefarious purpose.

He wore stained pants, ripped at his knees, and his
shoulder-length hair was rolled into dreadlocks. Unlike
the gang members, he carried no gun, which was of little consolation; he was as broad and muscular as them.

I wasn't sure what perverse thoughts he was thinking about me, a girl he'd found alone in the woods. I pulled my T-shirt away from my breasts.

"Whatever you're planning, it's not going to work," I said, straightening up to make myself appear bigger than I was. I eyed the three dead rabbits that were slung over the horse's neck, their feet bound with twine.

The boy glanced back at me and smiled. Despite his poor hygiene, his teeth were perfect—so straight and white. "And what is it that I'm planning? Really, I'd love to hear."

We were trotting down a highway now, the metal guardrails barely visible beneath the vines. Off in the distance was a half-crumbled bridge. "You want to have intercourse with me," I said matter-of-factly.

The boy laughed, a loud, raucous laugh, his hand slapping the horse's neck. "I want to have intercourse with you?" he repeated, as if he hadn't heard it right the first time.

"That's right," I said more loudly. "And I'll tell you now, I will not let that happen. Not even if . . ." I searched for the right metaphor.

". . . I was the last man on earth?" He looked out on the vast, unpopulated landscape and flashed a mischievous grin. His eyes were the pale green of grapes.

"Precisely." I nodded. I was glad he could at least speak and understand proper English. I wasn't having nearly as much trouble communicating as I would have imagined.

"Well that's good," the boy said. "Because I don't want to have intercourse with you anyway. You're not my type."

I laughed then too, until I realized he wasn't kidding. He kept his eyes straight ahead as he maneuvered the horse off the highway and onto a moss-covered street, urging it around holes in the pavement.

"What do you mean 'I'm not your type'?" I asked.

The plague had killed far more females than males. As one of the few women in The New America, especially an educated, civilized woman, I'd always supposed I was every man's type.

The boy glanced at me once and shrugged. "Eh," he muttered.

Eh? I was intelligent, I worked hard. I was told I was beautiful. I was Eve, the valedictorian of School. And all he could say was, *Eh?*

His shoulders shook a little. I looked at his face and realized, for the first time during our ride, that he was teasing me. He was making a joke.

"You find yourself very funny, don't you?" I asked, turning so he wouldn't see the sudden flush in my cheeks.

He tugged on the reins, directing the horse past the bridge and off toward the setting sun. As the sun went down it turned the sky the purplish-blue of bruises. Gray clouds were rolling in, accompanied by the distant boom of thunder.

"Well, you'd better be taking me back to where you found me now. My . . . very large man friend is waiting for me there. He's very scary and . . . kill-happy," I added, repeating the phrase I'd heard the gang use.

The boy kept chuckling to himself. "I am taking you back."

"Yes, I knew you were," I said, looking around. I wasn't quite sure where we were. We hadn't yet reached the WAL MA T. The road was nowhere in sight. Two yellowed poles shot up from the ground on our left, marking an old football field that was now thick with cornstalks.

"Is there anything you don't know?" the boy said, his face giving way to another smile. I turned away, pretending not to notice the dimple that formed in his right cheek, or the way his eyes shone brightly, like he was lit from within. The Illusion of Connection, Teacher Agnes had called it once. Was that what this was?

We were both silent for some time, listening to the

grumbling sky, until we turned into the neighborhood where I'd last seen Arden. I recognized a beaten tire swing, the rubber cracked in places. A wild cat roamed the street, its belly hanging low.

The boy scanned an overgrown front yard and pointed to a tiny figure, hidden behind some leaves. "I assume that is your 'very large man friend'?"

Arden slowly emerged from hiding. The knees of her pants were wet and muddy, like she'd been crawling on the ground.

I jumped off the horse's back, expecting her to question me, but she was too busy studying the boy to even acknowledge my presence. We were all silent for a moment, with only the horse's loud breathing filling the air. She kept one hand on her knife.

The boy shook his head. "You're paranoid too? Let me guess, you two are fresh out of School?" He dismounted in one swift motion. The sky rumbled again and he stroked the horse's neck, trying to comfort it. "Shhhh, Lila," he whispered.

"What do you know about School?" Arden asked.

"More than you'd think. I'm Caleb," he said, reaching out his hand for Arden to shake. She paused, staring at the mud caked under his nails and in the creases of his knuckles. Then, slowly, she relaxed her shoulders and let her grip slip from her knife. My eyes darted between them.

He was getting to her.

"Arden," I whispered, wishing she wasn't touching him. Her gaze settled on a tattoo on the front of his shoulder: a circle with The New American crest inside it. "Come on, let's go cook dinner." I knew this sudden male presence was as surprising to her as it was to me, but we couldn't stand there anymore, inches from him. Exposed. I started down the road, gesturing for Arden to follow. But she didn't move.

"I couldn't catch anything," she said, finally stepping away from Caleb. She looked at the three rabbits that hung from his horse's neck. Then she opened the sack that hung at her waist, showing me its empty insides.

The storm clouds were coming closer. A peal of thunder shook the air. I kicked a stone across the road, wishing I'd thought to take those rusty cans from the baby bear. Tonight would be another frigid, rainy night with nothing to eat.

Caleb climbed back onto his horse. "There's plenty of food at my camp if you two want to join."

I laughed at the suggestion, but Arden looked from me

back to Caleb, then at the rabbits.

"No . . ." I muttered under my breath. I grabbed her arm, tugging her back and away. Her feet were planted firmly in the dirt.

"What kind of food?" she asked.

"Everything. Boar, rabbit, wild berries. I killed a deer a few days ago." He gestured out at the gray horizon, his fingers stretching toward some unseen place. "It's less than an hour's ride."

I kept moving backward, step after step. But Arden's head was cocked, her fingers working at a knot in her short black hair. She strained against my grasp. "How do we know we can trust you?" she asked.

Caleb shrugged. "You don't. But you have no horse, nothing to eat, and a storm's coming. It might be worth a chance." Arden looked up at the gray sky, then back to the empty sack at her side.

After a moment she shook free from my grip. She circled the back of the horse and climbed on behind Caleb. "I'll take you up on that offer," she said, adjusting herself.

I shook my head, refusing to move. "No way. We're not going to your 'camp.'" I made quote signs in the air. It was surely a trap.

"Suit yourself. But I wouldn't want to be alone out

here if I were you. Especially not in this weather." Caleb pointed to the dense storm clouds, which were moving faster, stretching out, ready to spill water onto the forest. Then he turned the horse and they started down the road. Arden waved good-bye to me, not troubling to turn her head.

I looked back at the field we'd come through. The sunflowers leaned to one side, pushed down by the wind. I wasn't sure which direction the house was in, or how far off it was. I didn't know how to start my own fire, I didn't know how to hunt, and I didn't have a knife to call my own.

I dug my fingernails into my palm. "Wait!" I called, running after the horse. "Wait for me!"

eight

IT WAS THE DARKEST NIGHT I'D EVER SEEN, LIT ONLY BY flashes of lightning across the black sky. We'd been traveling for over two hours. I clung to Arden, grateful for the extra space between Caleb and me. As we made our way down a muddy road, I kept silent, reviewing all the ways we might die by Caleb's hand, or be manipulated into doing things we weren't supposed to. Among all the lies the Teachers had told us, there must have been some truths. After seeing the way the gang had skinned that animal alive, I knew men were as violent and callous as we had been told. I thought of the innocent Anna Karenina, and how she was oppressed by her husband, Alexei, and then seduced by her lover, Vronsky. Teacher Agnes had read her suicide scene aloud, shaking her head in disappointment. *If only she had known what you know*, she'd said. *If only.*

I would not be fooled. As soon as we arrived at Caleb's camp we'd eat, then wait out the storm. I wouldn't sleep. No, I'd stay awake and alert, my back against the wall. Then in the morning, when the sky had returned to its perfect cerulean blue, we'd be off. Me and Arden. Alone.

"So how'd you know about School?" Arden asked. She hadn't spoken much, except to question Caleb about the route he was taking.

I raised my cheek from Arden's back, suddenly interested in their conversation.

"I know more about Schools than I would like." Caleb kept his eyes on the road ahead. "I was an orphan, too."

"There are schools for boys then," Arden pressed. "I knew it. Where?"

"A hundred miles north. But they're not Schools, so much as labor camps. I know the things you've seen at School, I know how unspeakable it is, the girls who are being used for breeding. But I can tell you—" Caleb paused for a moment. He spoke slowly and matter-of-factly, like he'd known these secrets for years. "I can tell you that the boys have suffered, too, perhaps worse."

I couldn't stop from scoffing. It was always women who'd suffered at the hands of men. Men were the ones who'd started wars. Men had polluted the air and sea with smoke and oil, ruined the economy and filled the old prison systems up to their limits. But Arden reached over and pinched my thigh so hard I squealed. "You'll have to excuse her," she said. "She was the School valedictorian."

Caleb nodded, as if that explained some deeper truth about me. Then he leaned forward, urging the horse to pick up the pace. We galloped up a long incline, the crest of the hill just a quarter mile off. Trees stretched their limbs over the grassy terrain, creating menacing shadows. The rain was falling harder now. The drops felt like tiny pebbles hitting my skin.

"Oh no." Caleb stopped the horse in the mud. I followed his gaze. There, only a hundred yards ahead of us, was a government Jeep. Even through the rain, I could make out the two red taillights.

Caleb tried to turn the horse around, but it was too late. A beam of light stretched through the darkness, illuminating our faces.

"Stop! By order of the King of The New America!" a voice bellowed over a megaphone.

"Go," Arden urged. "Now!"

Caleb spun the horse around and we took off the way we'd come. I couldn't stop myself from looking back. The Jeep was spinning around, too, mud splashing from its back tires. It started toward us, our backs lit by the unblinking eyes of its front headlights.

"Stop in the name of the King! Or we will use force."

"No," I whispered to myself, clinging to Arden's slippery back. "No, this can't be happening." Maybe it was the downpour, or the mud, or the weight of the third person, but the horse was slower than before. The Jeep was gaining on us.

"We can't stay on this road," Caleb said. "They'll catch us." He pointed off to the side at a thickly wooded forest. The horse raced toward it. "Hold on!" Caleb shouted.

I gripped Arden desperately. The horse jumped off the side of the road and in seconds we were in the dense wood. The thick branches of trees whipped at my arms and back. "Keep your head down!" Caleb yelled.

The lights of the Jeep disappeared behind us. The vehicle had stopped on the road. "It's just a little farther," Caleb reassured us, as our bodies pitched and heaved over the uneven terrain. I didn't know what "it" was, but I hoped we would reach it soon.

The horse weaved in and out of the trees, finally coming to a stop in front of a nearly thirty-foot-wide river. Caleb jumped to the ground, helping Arden and me down. He slapped the horse's rear and she took off. For a moment the forest was quiet.

I glanced behind us. The Jeep's headlights lit the hazy night. The men slammed the car doors. "This way!" one of them yelled.

"Why are they after you?" I asked.

Caleb pulled us behind a boulder at the river's shore and we all crouched low. "They're not," he said. I looked up at him, confused. "They're after you." He retrieved a piece of paper from his back pocket.

Arden plucked it from his hands. There, staring back at us, was a black-and-white photograph of a girl with long, dark hair, and a plump, heart-shaped mouth. EVE, the paper read. 5'7", BLUE EYES AND BROWN HAIR. TO BE CAPTURED AND DELIVERED, ALIVE, TO THE KING. IF SEEN, ALERT THE NORTHWEST OUTPOST. Arden held it in her hands until a giant raindrop fell, splattering across my name.

Caleb peered around the boulder, to where the Jeep was idling. "I found it on the road this morning."

I grabbed the sheet from Arden's hand and stared back at my own face. It was my graduation photo—the only picture ever taken at School. Last month a woman from the government came and lined all thirty of us up outside, photographing us one by one. In the photo, I stood in front of the lake, the windowless building just visible in the background. "But why are they after me? Arden escaped, too."

Caleb looked down, his face half hidden by his matted brown hair. "What?" Arden asked. "What is it?"

He wiped the rain from his cheeks. "There's been talk from the City of Sand—we originally thought it was a rumor." Slowly, his eyes met mine. "The King wants an heir."

Arden shook her head. She kept staring at the photo. "Oh no . . ." she mumbled.

"What? What is it?" I asked, feeling panic swell in my chest.

She peered back to the road, where a few flashlight beams now canvassed the trees. "'*Eve has proven one of the best and brightest students we've seen at School. So beautiful, so smart, so obedient.*'" Headmistress Burns's words sounded different coming from Arden's mouth. Sinister, even. "That's what you get for your Medal of

Achievement, Eve. You weren't going to that building after all. You belong to the King."

My stomach was overcome by nausea. "What do you mean . . . *belong*?"

"You were going to bear his children, Eve." Arden practically laughed.

The King's pictures were in the hallways of our School. He was much older, with hair that was gray at the sides and dry, thin lips. Lines creased his forehead. I remembered Maxine had spoken of the King's supposed graduation visit. It suddenly seemed possible he really had been coming . . . for me.

"Of course you were. You're the perfect specimen. All that education, and all the Teachers' praise . . ." Arden went on, her fingers pressing against her temple.

I crumpled the poster in my hands. My breaths were short, my lungs tight. I didn't want to bear anyone's children—especially not the King's. But apparently the choice had already been made for me.

Caleb perched near the side of the boulder, his eyes fixed on the King's men. They made their way through the woods, the sounds of their boots crunching on leaves fill-ing the air. "We're not safe here," he said, looking behind him at the river. "Come—now." He darted toward the shore and waded into the rushing water, the rain hitting his bare back. Arden followed close behind. It took me a moment to realize: he wanted us to swim across.

I crouched down, frozen on the bank, as Arden dove under with ease. Behind me, the flashlights scanned the thick woods. The voices of the troops grew louder.

"Come on!" Caleb yelled. He paused, the water at his chest, letting Arden swim past. She kept swimming, coming up only for air.

Caleb rushed back to me on the shore. "Quick," he urged, grabbing my arm.

The river churned with white water. Arden moved downstream, swept away by the current. "I can't swim," I said, wiping my wet hair from my cheeks. My face crumpled as Arden struggled to the other shore. She was up, her clothes and backpack soaking, but unharmed.

"I don't know how," I said, my voice trembling. Behind us, the King's troops were getting closer, their flashlight beams reaching the water. "Just go," I choked out. I couldn't stop the sobs from coming now, my chest heaving with defeat. I pushed Caleb forward. "Go."

But he didn't move. He glanced back at the shadows in the forest, then at me, and then he grabbed my hand. "It's okay, Eve," he said.

I stopped crying, surprised by the warmth of his skin against my own. He was so close that I could feel each of his soft breaths. His green eyes were bright, illuminated by the sudden glow of the flashlight beam. "I'm not going to leave you."

CALEB PULLED ME FARTHER DOWN THE BANK, HIS HAND gripped tightly around mine. We sprinted over rocks and broken tree limbs. I could hear the men behind us, struggling in the dense wood.

"They're heading up the shore!" one yelled.

Caleb kept moving, seeming to sense every groove in the slippery stones, every patch of moss or rotten log. I watched his legs, careful to put mine down in the ghosts of his footsteps.

We rounded a bend and the flashlights disappeared. In the rain I could barely make out a structure in front of us, overturned on the shore. It looked like a giant dead cockroach. Caleb ran for it. I'd only seen a helicopter once before, in the pages of an archived book, but I recognized the bent propellers and podlike cockpit.

"Hurry—get in." He knocked out the shattered remnants of a window.

I lowered myself into its rusty shell and the shadows swallowed me whole. Caleb rushed in behind me, his feet crashing down on the floor. "They're coming," he whispered, as he pulled me into the front seats. The rain battered the cracked windshield, filling the cockpit with a relentless drumming.

"We need to hide," I said. My hands wandered over the copter's moldy insides. I felt a cushioned object, half my height—the passenger seat must have broken free in a crash. We crawled beneath it, the noise of the pelting rain muting our breaths.

In the dark, below the musty seat, I huddled beside Caleb, aware of the places where my body touched his. My shoulder pressed against his shoulder, the side of my leg against his. The closeness was alarming, but I didn't dare move away.

The troops' voices grew louder as they came down the bank. A flashlight beam hit the top of the copter and the broken glass sparkled. Caleb, barely visible in the beam's glow, pressed his fingers to his lips.

"They ran back through the woods. I'll search the shore and meet you on the road," a man said from close by. His flashlight came down into the helicopter, shining first on a pile of leaves. The beams ran along the dented wall and across the skeleton of the pilot, still strapped into the seat. It finally settled on my right shoe, the only part of me not hidden.

Go away, I thought, willing the beam off my foot. *It's nothing.* I closed my eyes and heard another voice, off in the distance, calling something out. It sounded like a question.

"No," the man replied after a moment. The flashlight disappeared from my foot. "Nothing." I heard footsteps beyond the windshield and then the forest was quiet. We stayed there, crouched underneath the broken seat, until the downpour let up.

"There might be food in here," Caleb said finally. He stretched his legs, then pushed the seat off us. "Help me look."

I felt around in the shadows, careful to stay away from the pilot's skeleton. After a while I found what felt like a rope and a large tin box.

"This?" I asked, passing it to Caleb.

He rifled through the box. There was a cranking noise and then a sudden light.

"Yes," he said, offering me a smile. "A lantern. See?" He grabbed the handle on the side and wound it, the light glowing brighter.

While he emptied the contents of the box onto the floor, sorting through tin cans and silver pouches, I studied his face. The river had washed away most of the dirt from his skin and it was now shiny and smooth, a few freckles covering the flat bridge of his nose. My eyes kept returning to his strong, angular features, the bones pressing against his skin. I knew I should be more afraid of him, but right now, I was simply fascinated. What was that word again, the one Teacher had used to describe her husband? The one Pip and I had joked about at School? Caleb, even with his brown nails and tangled hair, seemed almost . . . *handsome*.

He passed me a small silver pouch. "What are you smiling about?" he asked, raising one brow in a question.

"Nothing," I said quickly. I lifted the pouch to my lips and sucked down the warm water.

"You like being chased by armed troops?" He moved his hands over his tanned skin, wiping the rainwater from his arms, his shoulders, and his chest. "Is that your idea of fun?"

"Just forget it."

Caleb popped open a can of brown mush. "Or . . ." he began, licking the lid clean. "Were you smiling at *me*?"

"Definitely not." I watched as he brought the can to his mouth, and emptied its insides with his tongue. He chewed loudly, his lips falling open. Immediately the glimmer of handsomeness was gone.

I turned away. "Revolting," I murmured.

"This doesn't look appetizing to you? You can have the dehydrated peas then." He tossed me another pouch. I ate the dried pebbles in silence, but he continued staring at me. "So you and Arden . . ." He tilted his head to the side. ". . . friends? Or not so much?"

I popped another pea into my mouth and kept it there, waiting for it to soften. I could remember the exact moment I'd decided Arden was so unlike me that we could never be friends. We were running races in the yard. It was our sixth year at School and Pip had gotten her period that morning. She'd been insecure about wearing the pads that Dr. Hertz had given her, but Ruby and I had convinced her to come run, even if she didn't want to. As she stood near the lake, waiting for her turn, Arden yanked down her shorts.

Before that moment, I had given Arden so many chances. After she fought with Maxine in the bathroom, splitting her lip, I'd sworn it was an accident. I'd defended her to the other girls when she snapped at Teacher Florence, telling her that she wasn't her mother—that she already had one, alive, outside the walls, and she didn't need another. I'd even snuck her berries in the solitary room. But what she did to Pip was too much. *I bet you're real proud of yourself*, I'd yelled, as Pip took off toward the dormitories, eyes swollen and pink. *For one second of your life someone was more pathetic than you.* After that I'd made it clear to everyone how little I thought of her, how pitiful she'd always seemed to me. Soon no one spoke to Arden at all, really. Not even to hear stories of her mansion, or the parents who worked in the City.

I swallowed, the tasteless food finally soft enough to go down. "No . . . I wouldn't say we're friends."

Caleb sat against the back of the pilot's seat, scratching the back of his head. "So that's why she swam off, then. She doesn't give a—"

"No," I snapped. "Arden only cares about herself. She's always been that way."

Caleb stared at me for a moment, surprised. Then he set the empty cans back into the box. He poked his head out of the shattered window and looked around. "Well, we should stay here for the night. It might rain some more, and the troops won't be back in the area until it clears anyway. Maybe Arden will turn up tomorrow."

"She won't," I mumbled under my breath. I could hardly make Arden stay with me before. Now that she knew I had a target on my back, she was probably sprinting through the woods, desperate to put as much space between us as possible.

We pulled the thin silver blankets from the box and eased into opposite corners of the damp cockpit. "It'll only be a few hours till we set out again," Caleb added. "Don't be scared."

"I'm not," I assured him.

The lantern dimmed, then finally went out.

"Good," he said. But as he fell asleep, I thought again of the City of Sand and the man who waited for me there. The King had always been a comforting presence to us, a symbol of strength and protection. But his portrait at School felt menacing now, with his slack cheeks and the beady eyes that seemed always to follow me. Why had he chosen me, more than thirty years his junior, to breed? Why me, out of all the girls at School? The Teachers had spoken of him being the exception—the only man who could be trusted. It was yet another lie.

I knew the King would keep coming for me. I knew

he wouldn't stop. Not after the stories I'd been told about his unyielding commitment to The New America. Headmistress Burns had clasped her hands over her heart as she spoke of the way he'd saved people from uncertainty after the plague. He said we had no time for debate, that we must move relentlessly forward, without stopping. *One chance*, Headmistress had repeated, her eyes blurred by patriotic tears. *We only have one chance to rebuild.*

My clothes were still wet. I rung out the hem of my shirt and my pants, slowly, carefully, letting the water drip to the floor. When I was young Ruby ran after me through the halls once, pretending to be a monster with sharp claws and gnashing teeth. I screamed, ducking around trash bins and slamming through doors trying to escape. I begged her to stop, calling over my shoulder in panic, but she thought it too funny a joke. When she caught me, my chest was heaving. The game was so real. I never forgot the terror of being chased.

I pulled the thin blanket around my neck and closed my eyes, yearning for the comfort of my old bed, for the crisp sheets that were always pulled back, inviting me to sleep. I wished for the familiar smell of a venison dinner or the window seats in the library archives where Pip, Ruby, and I would sit, listening to the banned cassette of Madonna that was hidden behind *American Art: A Cultural History*. I felt the old battery-powered tape deck in my hand, the foam headphones on my ears as I tried to remember those lyrics, about the man on the island. I was thinking about Pip shimmying this way and that, in a secret dance, when I heard a noise outside.

I pushed farther back into the corner. Caleb was still asleep, his face slack with exhaustion. I heard it again—the cracking of tree branches.

"Caleb?" I whispered.

He didn't wake up.

I closed my eyes as the noise came closer and covered my face with the blanket, my body stiff with fear. Rustling. The snap of twigs. The unmistakable squish of footsteps in the mud. When I pulled the blanket from my face my breaths stopped. I couldn't move. A figure was standing outside the copter, only a few feet away, silhouetted by the moon.

They were looking directly at me.

ten

THE BLANKET FELL FROM MY FACE. I DIDN'T DARE REACH for it, didn't dare move, for fear of being seen. On the other side of the cockpit, Caleb turned over, rocking the giant metal shell. The figure took another step forward and rested a hand on the broken doorframe. I winced, already sensing what was coming: the cold gun that would be pulled from his belt, the handcuffs that would pinch my wrists.

"Eve?" a familiar voice finally whispered.

I peered up through the shattered window. Arden's clothes were soaked and her black hair was slicked to her head. In the pale light I could see her face, strained with worry. "Are you there? Are you okay?"

"Yes, it's me." I moved into the moonlight. "I'm fine."

She climbed into the copter, her boots sinking into the leaves. She glanced from me to Caleb's curled up body, as if a question in her mind had at last been answered. Then she settled down in a seat.

"You came back . . ." I cranked the plastic lantern, staring at Arden. She was shaking from the cold, dripping as if she'd emerged again from the river. I handed her my blanket.

Arden dug through the box, ripping open a packet of dried food. "Well," she shrugged, "I *do* need to eat." She nibbled on a dehydrated carrot, already ignoring me.

"Were you"—I leaned in as I spoke—"*worried* about me?"

Arden stopped eating. She glanced over her shoulder again at Caleb. "No," she said quickly. "I just didn't know if you were safe with him."

I wanted to tell her that if she was concerned about my safety then technically the answer was *yes*, she *was* worried about me, but I restrained myself. As I took in Arden's drenched clothes, I wondered if I'd misjudged her. If there was more to her than the girl who'd insisted all those years that she'd rather eat alone than spend time with the rest of us.

She threw down the empty silver pouches and let out a quick burp. "I suppose you want your blanket back?" she asked, handing it to me. It stayed there for a moment, a silver curtain between us.

I shook my head. "You keep it."

The lantern dimmed, its charge waning. Arden's pale face was the last thing I saw before the light went out and I fell asleep.

———‖———

THE NEXT MORNING CALEB BEAT BACK THE TALL GRASS in front of us, clearing a path with a stick. We'd waited for his horse to return to the bank, but when the sun rose we had to leave.

"It's a day's walk from here," he said. "With a little luck we'll make it to camp before nightfall." We moved along a moss-covered street. The sun had broken free from the yellowy-pink dawn and now the sky was bathed in white.

"We can't stay at the camp long," I said, falling back to confer with Arden. "We can get supplies but then we have to start on our way to Califia."

The encounter with the King's troops still played in my mind. Even in these early hours of morning, with no signs of the Jeep, I glanced over my shoulder every few yards. I flinched at the harsh cries of birds overhead.

Arden swatted a fly that circled her. "You don't need to tell me," she muttered, and then coughed—a wet, phlegmy sound. "Does this trail get any easier?" she asked, pushing a prickly branch away from her face.

"We should hit a neighborhood soon." Caleb ducked under a low limb. "Careful." He looked up at the sky again, as he'd been doing all day.

Before we'd set off, Arden and I had waited while he fiddled with sticks in the dirt, measuring their shadows with the passing minutes. Then he knew where to go, as if he'd been communing with the earth in a strange language we couldn't understand.

"You're watching it like a clock," I said now, pointing to the sun.

"It *is* my clock. And my compass and my calendar." He brought his finger to his chin to feign surprise. "Seems like there are some things you don't know after all . . ."

I glanced behind me, to Arden. She was picking at the dirt beneath her fingernails, oblivious. I knew Caleb was our best bet for safety. He had stayed with me at the river, hiding me in the fallen helicopter, for what reason I couldn't be sure. I still didn't understand his motivations, or believe we could trust him completely. I didn't like the way he always seemed to be mocking me, or how he pressed me last night with questions I didn't want to answer.

"Look, *Caleb*," I said, enunciating his name. "We appreciate your help. But we never asked for it."

"Yes," Caleb said. "You reminded me of that. An hour ago . . . and this morning . . . and when you agreed to come back to camp. You'll stay a night, take our food, then I am to escort you back to Route eighty so you can move on to Califia. I got it."

He led us down another road, which dead-ended into a row of decrepit houses. Floodwaters had swept through, leaving a brown ring on the shingles a foot above the front doors. A message was spray painted across a brick facade: DYING. PLEASE HELP.

"Who's hungry?" Caleb asked.

Before we could answer, he bounded up the splintered front steps and disappeared into the house.

"Guess this is our lunch stop . . ." Arden murmured, following him.

Inside, the floorboards were warped and broken. Mold bloomed black on the walls. I covered my nose with my T-shirt, trying to block out the smell. In the corner of the room was a giant frame of sorts, its shattered front creating a design like a star.

"What's that?" I asked, pointing to it.

Caleb moved through the living room, stepping over waterlogged books and mounds of putrid, rotting garbage. Arden and I slowly followed.

"A television," he said, as we reached the doorway to the kitchen.

I nodded, but I only vaguely recognized the term. The center of it looked like it could've contained something valuable. The rotted sofa was facing it, as if a whole family sat there to stare at it.

Every cabinet in the kitchen was open, the cupboards strewn with dirty plastic forks and empty cans. A few chairs lay on the floor, their seats ripped, exposing mildewed gray insides. The ceiling was falling down in clumps.

"Careful," Arden hissed, pulling me to her. She pointed to a hole in the floor I'd nearly stepped through.

Caleb jumped over the gap and headed toward a staircase, which led into a dark cellar. "I'll check to see if there's anything in the basement."

While Arden wandered back through the living room, I approached the refrigerator in the corner. It was covered with old photos and drawings. One picture was of a young couple, a baby cradled in their arms. The woman's bangs were stuck to her sweaty forehead, but the light caught her wide, sparkling eyes. Below it was a colorful drawing of a stick figure family. All three people—mother, father, and child—were surrounded by ominous ghosts, their outlines scribbled in black crayon.

In those last days, I drew as much as I could. I'd sit downstairs at my plastic blue table and go through a stack of paper, drawing for my mother. I drew her pictures of us in the old playground by our house, the one with the tilt-a-whirl where she spun me around and around and around. I'd draw her in bed and the doctor, a magic wand perched in his hand as he made her well. I showed her our house, with a fence around it to keep the bad virus out. I slipped them under her door so she could have them—her special gifts. *Kisses*, she would say, patting the other side of the wood. *I would give you a million kisses if I could.*

I glanced at the young woman's face one last time before turning to the empty room. I heard a creak somewhere above me, and followed it.

"Arden?" I called, walking down the silent hallway. The floor groaned with each step. The cool breeze rushed in through the broken windows. "Where are you?"

I peered into a tiny bathroom, its floor pitted from

missing tiles. "Arden?" I called. My voice echoed.

At the end of the hall a door was slightly ajar. I headed toward it, passing by another bedroom with a rotted bed, the springs popping out of the frame.

I crept closer, easing my way along the wall. The wallpaper was peeling in sections, scraping at my bare shoulders. My pulse quickened and the small of my back beaded with sweat. We'd entered the house in haste, but we should've searched it before splitting up. There was always the chance that we were being watched.

The door was cracked. I looked inside. It was a child's room, with a chest of dusty toys and bright blue walls. A few ragged stuffed animals sat on the miniature bed. I walked in, picking up a one-armed teddy bear that looked like it had been worn in long before the plague struck.

It happened so quickly. I heard footsteps behind me. My body hit the ground with a thud. I screamed out as a figure in a clown mask held me down, its crooked, crimson smile taunting me.

"Please don't kill me!" I screamed. "Please!"

The clown paused for a moment, its hands pinning my shoulders to the splintered floor. Then I heard choked giggling. Arden pulled the mask off and fell over, her body shaking with laughter.

"What is wrong with you?" I yelled, hopping to my feet. "Why would you do that?"

Caleb appeared in the doorway, his face blanched. "What happened? I heard you scream." He gripped one rusty can in each hand.

I pointed at Arden, who rolled on her side, letting out deep, throaty laughs. She wiped her eyes with the hem of her shirt. "Arden scared me. On purpose. That's what happened."

Caleb glanced from her back to me. His mouth hung open but no words came out. My heart thumped hard in my ribcage.

"It's not funny," I finally managed. "I could have had a knife. I could have killed you!" I paced back and forth, smacking one hand against the other for emphasis. She kneeled, her back arched and her face toward the floor. "Arden—look at me. Would you just turn around and look at me?" I yelled.

Caleb grabbed my arm, pulling me back.

But Arden kept her head down, her black bob a mess of tangles. She was writhing. Her palm banged on the floor.

"Arden?" I said again, softer this time. Her eyes were squeezed shut, her cheeks pink and contorted.

She turned over, her chest heaving. I stood, reaching out my hand, but she didn't move. Instead her body curled into a tight ball, tensing with great effort. She hacked loudly, her coughs splitting the air. I dropped to the floor. My hand rested on her back as she lurched forward, trying to free her lungs. When she pulled away we both looked down.

Her palms were covered with blood.

eleven

"SHE WAS SOAKED THROUGH LAST NIGHT," I TOLD CALEB when we finally reached the woods outside of his camp. With each mile Arden's coughs had grown louder, her gait slower, until she could not walk anymore. Caleb and I had taken turns pulling her along in a wagon we'd found, RADIO FLYER scrawled across its side. One minute her teeth chattered and the next she was hunched over the wagon's side, trying to expel the bloody phlegm from her lungs. Arden had managed to fall asleep, her body hugging the scavenged cans of food. "It must be from the river and the rain."

"I knew a boy who was sick like this once," Caleb said.

We hoisted her up, wrapping her arms around each of our shoulders.

"And what happened?" I asked. Caleb didn't answer. "Caleb?"

"It's probably different," he said. But his face looked tense, even in the faded light of the night sky.

"I'm fine," Arden mumbled, trying to straighten up. The corners of her mouth were caked with dried spit.

We made our way through the dense gray woods, the leaves tickling my neck as we went. Animals rustled in the brush. In the distance, a wild dog pack howled, hungry for their next meal. Finally the forest spilled out into a clearing, revealing the most dazzling sight I'd ever seen. There, before us, was a giant lake, its inky surface reflecting thousands of stars.

"Lake Tahoe," Caleb said.

I looked up, studying the twinkling white clusters. Some were so bright they looked almost blue. Others faded into the distance like shimmery dust.

"It's magnificent." But that word didn't come close to describing the awe I felt then, dwarfed in the presence of the sky. "Look, Arden." I nudged her arm. I wished I had my paints and brushes, so that I could try to capture even the faintest impression of the scene.

There was only us, the black ring of land, and that brilliant dome.

But Arden only winced in pain.

"Where is the camp?" I asked, my awe giving way to dread. "We need to get her inside."

"You're looking at it," Caleb said. He approached the steep, muddy incline covered in weeds and fallen branches.

I watched in confusion as Caleb grabbed a rotted log nestled into the dirt and tugged, revealing a large board the size of a door. He swung it open. Past it was a black hole, burrowed deep into the side of the mountain. "Come on," he said, gesturing me inside.

My stomach quaked. My head felt light. Staring into the blackness, my fears returned. It was already so risky to be out in the wild with Caleb. I hadn't imagined the camp as an underground lair. Aboveground, I could always take off running. But down in the dark . . .

I took a step back. "No . . ." I muttered under my breath. "I can't."

"Eve." Caleb offered me his hand. "Arden needs help—now. Come inside. We aren't going to hurt you."

Arden shivered at my side. She coughed and opened her eyes just long enough to say something that sounded like "listen." She leaned on me as I guided her into the dim tunnel, my hands trembling. Caleb closed the door behind me.

"Come this way," he said, ducking under Arden's other arm to help me carry her. As we moved in the dark, the cold dirt wall brushed against my shoulder. The ground was solid beneath my feet.

"This tunnel—you found it?" I asked, my voice echoing in the hollow cavity.

Caleb made a sharp right and took us down another tunnel, sensing the path in the dark. "We made it." Far ahead, I could hear the sounds of a gathering. Distant murmuring, the clatter of pans, some faint hoots.

"You built this into the mountain?" I asked. Arden coughed again, her feet limp beneath her.

Caleb said nothing for a long while. "Yes." I could hear him breathing as we walked. "After the plague, I was taken to a makeshift orphanage, in an abandoned church. Kids—boys and girls—were sleeping on pews and in closets, sometimes five of us all huddled together to keep warm. I only remember one adult—the woman who opened the cans of food for us. She called us the 'leftovers.' After a few months the trucks showed up and took the girls to Schools. The boys went to camps—labor camps—where we built things all day, every day." Each word was clipped. He kept his eyes on the ground in front of us.

"When did you escape?" I asked. We moved through the tunnel, toward a light that glowed brighter as we neared it.

"Five years ago. The excavation was just starting when I got here," Caleb answered. I wanted to know more, about who was organizing it and how, but I was afraid to press him further.

We turned and the passage emptied out into a wide, circular room, with a fire pit in the center. The cavern reminded me of an animal's burrow. The mud walls were embedded with fat gray stones and four other tunnels snaked out from this expansive center. Before we could take another step, an arrow whizzed by my face, nearly clipping my ear.

"Watch where you're going!" A boy with large, ropy muscles laughed. He walked over to the wall beside us, where two giant circles were etched, forming a target. His eyes were locked on me as he pulled the arrow out with one good yank.

A pack of boys was gathered around the fire, their chests bare. When they spotted Caleb they hollered wildly.

"We were wondering where you were," a boy with a

dome of thick black hair called out. They pounded their fists to their chests in some primitive welcome. My spine stiffened as the boys turned to stare at me.

"At least hunting was a success," the one with the arrow hissed. He scanned my bare legs, the long-sleeved shirt that hung loosely over my breasts. I crossed my arms in front of me, wishing I was more covered. "Look what we got here, boys! A lady . . ." He stepped toward me, but Caleb pressed his palm out to stop him from moving any closer.

"Enough, Charlie," Caleb warned.

Two others, about fifteen, carried a wild boar in from a side tunnel. They set their quarry on the ground, releasing a gush of clotted blood from the animal's insides.

"Does Leif know about this?" one asked. He was tall and thin, a cracked pair of glasses sitting askew on his nose.

"He will soon enough," Caleb replied.

One boy knelt beside the boar carcass. He ran two knife blades against each other, letting out a sharp, scraping sound that made the hair on my arms bristle. His eyes wandered over Arden's body, and then, when he'd had his fill, he started on the boar, hacking at its neck. Bits of bone flew into his face. It was savage, the way his knife landed again and again at the place where its head met its body. I winced with every blow.

The boy didn't stop until the head split off and rolled across the floor. The boar stared at me, its pupils covered in a gray film. I wanted to run through the corridor, back the way we'd come, not stopping until the open air embraced me. But I felt Arden limp at my side, and reminded myself why we were here. As soon as she was better we'd be gone, away from this dank dugout with these boys who looked at me as though I were something to be devoured.

A hefty one with blond, matted hair threw some more wood on the fire. He inspected Arden's slight frame. "They can stay in my room," he laughed. I gripped Arden tightly. "I'd be happy to share my bed."

"They're not staying in anyone's room," a gruff voice interrupted. "They're not staying at all."

An older boy appeared from one of the tunnels beyond the fire. He was wearing long shorts that hung past his knees and his chest sprouted dark curls. His black hair was pulled into a bun, revealing thick, crisscrossing scars on the top of his back. A group of older boys emerged in a line behind him, spilling out into the room. My skin prickled with fear. There were ten more of them at least, all taller and wider than me. And they looked angry.

"This isn't good," Arden breathed.

Caleb placed himself between us and them. "It isn't a debate, Leif. I found them in the woods. She was attacked by a bear." I looked down at the dirt floor, trying to avoid the stares. "They need to stay here."

Leif's eyes were deep brown, their edges lined with a thick curtain of black lashes. "It's too dangerous. You know how the King is about the sows. He's probably looking for them already." He came toward us, his face only two feet from Caleb's. He was so close I could see the bits of leaves buried in his hair and the smears of ash on his tense, muscular arms.

"Sows?" Arden whispered, her breath hot on my neck. "That's what we are?"

"That may be what we're *called*," I answered. "But that's not what we are."

The band of boys circled us. The pack closed us in, blocking our escape route. Arden coughed, her body heaving with the effort.

"She's sick?" a gap-toothed boy asked, his face softening. I noticed a tattoo on his shoulder—a circle with The New American crest inside it. It was the same one Caleb had, in the same exact place. I looked around, noticing that all the boys were tattooed.

"Very," I said. They retreated at the word, breaking into whispers, a short, chubbier one muttering something that sounded like "plague." Arden's head lolled to the side and rested on my shoulder.

Caleb's eyes were still locked with Leif's. "If we throw them out she'll die. I won't have it."

The corner of Leif's lip curled up in displeasure, reminding me of a snarling dog. "They have to stay in the west room, away from the others," he finally said. Arden was barely able to look up, so he instead fixed his narrow, almost-black eyes on me. "You are not to go above-ground without permission. And you are to stay out of our way. Do you understand?"

Leif glanced at the boy beside him, who carried a short stack of bowls. As if instinctually, the boy kneeled down, filling two from a pot of beans that rested near the fire. Then he handed them to Leif. I stepped forward. Leif's massive shoulders were nearly level with my eyes. He handed me a bowl. I grabbed it but he didn't let go, his fingers still clutching it.

"Welcome," he said in a voice that made it clear we were anything but. He held me there, in his gaze, his eyes roaming over my face until they lowered to my breasts, my waist, my legs. I felt a rush of panic and pulled at the bowl, trying to get free. He released his grip suddenly, sending me stumbling backward. The beans sloshed down the front of my shirt. Another boy let out a loud, callous laugh.

I dabbed at the stain, my cheeks hot and red. It wasn't enough that I was unprotected in this camp, it wasn't enough that Leif terrified me. He had to humiliate me, too.

"Come on," Caleb said, taking Arden's dinner from Leif. "I'll show you where you'll stay." He wrapped an arm around Arden's side, and we started down a tunnel illuminated by rows of flashlights set into the dirt floor. "So that is Leif," Caleb whispered.

I turned back as Leif angrily kicked aside the boar's head. The boys resumed their activities. The large one launched another arrow, two skinnier boys wrestled, and a few others worked feverishly to skewer slabs of meat onto sharpened sticks. I thought at once of *Lord of the Flies*, and the day Teacher Florence read the scene where Simon is murdered by the pack of wild boys, citing Gang Mentality as the motivation. *It is when they're isolated, encouraged only by one another's violence, that men are the most dangerous,* she'd said, sitting on the edge of her desk, the book open in her lap.

Remembering the chorus of hoots, the eyes that shame-lessly roamed my body, the whispering between them, I knew: some things she'd told us *were* true. Even now.

twelve

"MORE?" I ASKED, HOLDING THE SPOONFUL OF BEANS IN front of Arden's cracked lips. She mumbled something that sounded like "no," then rolled back onto her side, kicking the quilt off her mottled legs. Her eyes fell closed.

It had been like this all night. She'd wake occasionally, asking for water or food, then crumple back onto the sunken mattress. Sometimes she twisted in pain, complaining of an ache that shot up her spine. Caleb had dragged in a tub filled with lake water, and I'd kept her awake long enough to wash the sweat from her skin and pick the leaves from her hair with a broken comb.

The dirt cavern was off one of the main tunnels, a cramped room with only a mattress and a desk covered with yellowed children's books. I had searched its drawers wishing, against all logic, to find medicine. I had never quite realized its value before. At School they seemed to have a limitless supply.

We took it for granted, the ease with which anything—a cough, an infection, skin sliced on a broken lantern—was treated. A pill here, a shot to numb the flesh before stitches, sweet bubble-gum-pink syrup dripping down your throat. When Ruby seized up in the yard, overcome by a knifing pain in her side, she was whisked away and emerged days later, black twine marking her abdomen where her appendix had been cut out. *What would have happened, in the wild?* we'd wondered aloud as we inspected that scar. Maxine guessed she would've had to take it out herself, probably with rusty scissors. *No*, Headmistress corrected. She'd been walking behind our table in the dining hall, making sure we'd swallowed down the last of our vitamins. *She simply would have died.*

I brushed back Arden's thick black hair, feeling the heat of her skin. I remembered the first time I saw her.

In those years following the plague new students arrived regularly, some found in the woods, some dropped off by adults who could no longer provide for them. She was the tall girl in the faded blue dress who had appeared at School three years after I had, an eight-year-old rushed in through the side gate. She stayed in a quarantine room for a month, alone, as we all did when we first arrived. Pip and I had huddled by the tiny glass window in the door, watching while she brushed her teeth. She spit the white foam into the trash can and we wondered aloud if she seemed any different. It was a game among the students. We all paused there whenever we walked down the hallway, looking for the telltale blue bruises to appear beneath the skin's surface. We waited for the whites of her eyes to turn a phlegm-colored yellow. They never did.

Arden rolled over and moaned, a deep guttural noise that terrified me. She sounded so much like my mother had in those final days. Now, in that dank room, I ran down a mental list of my mother's symptoms. Arden had lost some weight, but it wasn't severe. She didn't have nosebleeds and her legs did not swell and weep, swell and weep, leaving puddles around her feet. Yet the way Arden hacked, the way she shook with chills, the way her eyes rolled back so I could see only the whites . . .

I squeezed her cold hand, willing her to shoot up in bed, awake and more alive than ever. To tell me to quit hovering and dismiss me with a roll of her eyes. But nothing. Only another kick of the leg, another moan. I said the words I couldn't have said to my mother, the words that curdled in my throat that day in July when the trucks came through the barricade, the words that had since lodged there, near my heart, turning to something solid.

I was five again, my steps light on the stairs. She'd stopped waiting for the doctors, had heard the reports that they would only help the rich. She'd opened the door to her room. I went to hug her but she'd put the plastic over my mouth and dragged me to the street, calling with her broken voice, calling out for them to stop. I tried to hold onto the mailbox as she ran back, afraid to even kiss me. I tried to keep my arms around its wooden post but I was loaded up and onto the bed of the truck, my body limp in the old woman's grasp.

"Please," I begged Arden now, closing my eyes, rocking with the sound of my own voice. I squeezed her hand again, turning it over. "Don't leave me. I need you."

When Arden didn't stir I returned my head to my

pillow and welcomed the tears. She might never get better. We might never be back on the road, together, heading to Califia.

———•••———

HOURS LATER, I AWOKE TO A BLINDING LIGHT.

Someone hovered in the doorway of the room, pointing a flashlight at my face. The silhouette shifted and the beam dropped to the ground. I rubbed at my eyes, trying to make sense of the tiny figure before me; the person could not have been any taller than my hip. Shaggy hair came down to her shoulders, and the wide, fluffy expanse of a tutu spread out around her waist.

I blinked in the darkness, but the figure was still there—real—not the shadowy remnant of a dream.

"What's your name?" I whispered to the little girl, waiting for my vision to adjust to the dark. She took a step backward. "Come here, come to me." I lifted my arm to signal her over. But before I could say anything more she darted away, down the dimly lit corridor.

I sat up in bed, fully awake now. I didn't know how a little girl had found her way to this all-male camp, but I knew I had to follow her. I raced toward the threshold, watching as she padded down the tunnel, barely visible in the flashlight beams.

"Wait!" I called. "Come back!"

She disappeared around a sudden bend.

I looked down the empty hall. The tunnel wound around and I followed it, trying to keep away from the black holes on either side where the boys slept. She was still ahead of me, winding through the corridor, her tutu bobbing up and down as she ran. The tunnel split and she turned suddenly, darting down an unlit path. I followed after her, my legs pumping fast.

"I'm not going to hurt you," I whispered urgently. "Please, stop!"

I dashed quickly, easily, my steps lighter than they'd been in days. It felt good to be up, to be moving, and with each yard I sprinted my mind quieted, leaving only the sound of my own breaths. Before long I could see the shadowy figure in front of me, steps ahead. Then the tunnel twisted once more and opened up beneath the star-dusted sky.

She ran into the trees, letting out a raspy shriek as though it was a funny game. I kept pace until she raced around the other side of the hill and plowed under a wide expanse of tall bushes. I leaned over to breathe, the effort catching up with me. When I finally raised my head, I realized she was gone. I was alone. In the dark. Outside the dugout.

I couldn't go farther; it would be foolish to wander the woods, following the girl over the hills. If I could get back inside the tunnel I could find Caleb, tell him that she had gotten out and was on her own. But turning around, I saw only shadows. I started back toward the trees, but the forest was thick. Leaves rustled beneath my feet. Branches cracked above me. When I reached the place where I thought the exit had been there was no hill, only a rocky incline leading down to the lake.

I spun around and ran toward the opposite side of the forest, my breath quickening. I recalled the moment by the river, the rain hard on my skin, the troops coming at me with their guns in hand. I saw Caleb's back in front of me, the face on the flyer, the words Arden had spoken aloud: *You belong to the King.* How could I have been so stupid to leave the dugout, to go out in the middle of the night, with the soldiers still after me? I had been warned.

Ahead, a cliff towered ten feet over my head. I was running so fast that I nearly collided into it. I must have been on the backside of the hill, but it was too dark to be certain. I took off alongside the cliff, hoping to circle up to the mossy mound that contained the entrance, when I heard something behind me. I had no time to turn, no time to run. In an instant, a strong hand came down upon my arm.

"What the hell are you doing here?" Leif hissed, jerking me forward. His contorted face was barely visible in the scattered starlight. I tried to wriggle out of his hold, but he squeezed tighter. "I told you not to leave the dugout."

"I know," I managed, wincing at the pain in my wrist. "I'm sorry." I didn't dare say more. I didn't dare breathe.

"Who said you could go out?" He snapped. His top lip was raised in disgust, revealing a chipped front tooth. "Did Caleb tell you?"

"No—I was following a little girl. She ran outside and disappeared somewhere over there, but I—"

"A little girl?" Leif laughed, but it sounded more like a snarl. "There are no little girls in the camp."

"You're hurting me," I said, but his hand remained closed around my delicate wrist.

He yanked me forward, his footsteps falling loudly on the path. "It was stupid of you to come out here. There's a reason I'm on watch duty. We're most vulnerable during these hours—especially with you here."

"I know," I said, hating his grip on me. As he pulled me toward the other side of the hill, I could feel the blood cooling in my hand, beyond the dam where his fingers pressed down to my bone.

Finally he released my wrist. He felt around the side of a mossy mound, and my stomach quaked thinking of what he might do to me. But then he tugged on a log, revealing another entrance to the dugout.

"I saw the troops tonight," he said slowly, so that I could process each word. "Haven't seen them in this area for months. But there they were, walking along that ridgeline." He gestured to a mountain beyond the trees.

He waited for me to say something—to react, to apologize maybe, but when I opened my mouth no words came out.

"Go on, get inside," he growled. "We wouldn't want anything to happen to our precious Eve, now would we?" His eyes were cool black marbles buried in his skull.

"No," I said, turning from his gaze. "We wouldn't." I ducked into the tunnel, relieved to be free of him.

"Yours is the doorway on the right, three away," he said as the moss-covered slat came down behind me, sealing me in the narrow corridor once again.

When I reached the cavern, I was thankful to see Arden's familiar face glowing in the fading flashlight. Still, I shook, my hands trembling, my heart banging in my chest. He'd recited where my room was so quickly. Too quickly.

I listened for echoes in the tunnel, my spine stiff against the cold wall, afraid those beady black eyes would come when I least expected it, to find me.

thirteen

CALEB AND I RODE THROUGH THE WOODS, WINDING IN AND
out of trees. After the sighting of the troops the previous night,
the oldest boys had been on watch all day, making sure the
soldiers had left the area. No one spoke to me, no one dared
look at me. It wasn't until they'd discovered fresh tire tracks
on the road leading away from the lake that the lockdown
had ended. Caleb had appeared in our doorway while I was
tending to Arden and invited me to hunt with him. I didn't
mind that I had to wear boy's clothing—ripped cotton shorts
and a loose shirt—or tie my hair back in disguise. I was just
thankful to be out in the fresh air, away from that dank cave.
Away from the underground lair and that animal, Leif.

When we reached a grassy clearing Caleb scanned the tree line, gazing down at the rocky shore. "Nothing there." He turned the horse around. "We'll have to find a lookout point."

The sky was a deep orange with billowing clouds, their bellies traced with red. We'd tracked a wild boar across a field and into a quarry, until it was startled by a falling rock. Now we were on the lookout for deer. I slid back on the horse, trying to enjoy the freedom of being aboveground. But last night's encounter still consumed my thoughts.

"Your friend Leif . . ." I began, trying to piece together Caleb's relationship with him—how he could live and work, day in and day out, with such a brute. I'd met Caleb two days ago and he'd yet to do anything I could deem suspicious. He hadn't left me at the river. He'd brought Arden and me breakfast and lunch, towels and fresh rainwater to bathe in. He'd even swept the room for us when we were sleeping. "He's quite the charmer," I finished, unable to hide the edge in my voice.

Caleb kept his eyes on the rocky cliff ahead of us, his sheath of arrows swinging on his shoulder. "I'm sorry he scared you last night. He was furious about the soldiers." One hand moved over the horse's neck, combing out the knots in her thick black mane. "He's convinced you made up that story about the little girl. There's no reasoning with him."

"Why would I lie about that? I saw her," I said to Caleb's back. "I was alone out there, and he practically threatened me."

Caleb shook his head as we climbed the side of the hill, the horse's uneven steps pitching us from one side to another. He didn't think I'd seen a little girl either, but he believed I'd seen *someone*. "Leif wasn't always like that. He used to be"—Caleb paused, searching for the right word—"better."

We ducked under a low branch. "That's hard to imagine." The leaves brushed over my spine as I ducked forward, careful to keep a space between us.

Caleb grew quiet. "Leif was funny, once," he finally said. "Really funny. We'd spend all day deconstructing buildings, brick by brick, and loading the materials onto trucks to be hauled to the City of Sand. Leif used to make up these songs while we worked." Caleb looked over his shoulder, his cheeks ruddy with a sudden smile.

"What songs? What are you laughing about?"

He turned back around. "You don't want to know."

"Try me."

"Fine. But don't say I didn't warn you." He cleared his throat in mock seriousness. "My," he crooned, his voice completely out of tune, "balls are sweating, my balls are sweating, I can't keep my balls from sweating, noooo, noooo, noooo!"

I leaned in, noticing the folds at the corner of his eyes and the faint brown spots that covered the top of his cheekbones. "Why is that funny? What are 'balls'? Like the ball of your foot?"

Caleb pulled at the reins of the horse and fell forward, his back heaving up and down with laughter.

"What? What is it?" I asked.

It took a moment for him to compose himself. "It's . . ." he said, his face crumpled. "Like these things that . . ." he paused, as if deep in thought, and then shook his head suddenly. "No, I'm sorry, I can't. It's just funny, Eve. Trust me."

I wanted to press him until he answered the question, but something told me the joke would be better left unexplained.

The horse plodded up the rest of the hill and onto a landing. The lake stretched out before us, reflecting the tangerine sky. From up high we could see the field where we'd found the boar, patches of woods, and a rocky strip of beach.

"There they are," Caleb said, pointing to the herd of deer drinking at the water's edge. Even from the cliff I could make out their golden coats and the horns that reached toward the treetops.

Caleb guided the horse back down the path. "So what happened to him?" I finally asked, when we were halfway to the woods. "To Leif?"

Caleb's agile body moved with the horse's, as if they were one. I watched the back of his gray T-shirt, focusing on a spot where the cloth split at the seams. I had the sudden urge to reach out and touch it, but I kept my hands firmly on Lila. "Leif had a twin brother then. Asher. Anything you said, they would always glance sideways at each other before responding, like Leif was checking what Asher would do first, or Asher was deciding whether to laugh." We started back through the woods, down to the rocky shore. "We went to work one day and Asher was sick. Looking back, I don't think it was anything major, it couldn't have been. But the guards were terrified. It was only a few years after the plague." He buried his hand into his brown hair. "When we came back his bunk was empty. He was gone."

"He died?" I asked. The horse shifted beneath me and I stroked her side, suddenly thankful for her calm, warm presence.

"No." Caleb shook his head. "They took him into the woods and left him there."

"Who?"

"The guards. They pinned his legs down with rocks. We could hear them bragging that night, about how they'd saved us all from the return of the plague."

I brought my hand to my mouth, imagining one of the boys at camp, alone in the woods, sick, with his legs pressed to the ground.

"It was like something inside of Leif broke. I never saw him—the old him—again. He was a different person after that night." Caleb dismounted and drew his bow and arrow, moving slowly toward the deer at the shore. A few raised their heads, but seeing Caleb, so calm, so still, they turned back toward the water.

He took a few more steps before aiming at a doe off to the side. The arrow left the bow and a moment later plunged deep into the deer's fleshy neck. The other animals scattered as the doe staggered back, stunned. Within seconds, Caleb released another arrow, which hit her in the side. Panicked, she ran into the water, then struggled back up the shore, a trail of blood in her wake.

"Stop!" I cried, scrambling off the horse, my eyes fixed on the wounds in her neck and side. "She's in pain."

Caleb approached her, his steps unhurried. "It's okay," he said softly to the doe. He took the animal's neck in his hands and unsheathed his knife. "It's going to be all right." Then he whispered something to her, over and again, which seemed to ease the panic. He brought his knife to her neck. In one swift motion he slit her throat, and the blood spilled out onto the pebbled shore, clouding the lake water red.

The tears came hot and fast, my body shaking as I watched life leave the animal's eyes.

I had grown up with death. I'd seen it all around me in the faces of neighbors, hauling sleeping bags into their backyards for burial. I'd seen it beyond the car window, in the lines of people rioting outside the pharmacies, their skin mottled and red. I'd seen it in my own mother, standing on the front porch, blood dripping from her nose.

But for twelve years, inside that School, I had been safe. The walls protected me, the doctors were there to cure us, I wore the warning whistle around my neck. As Caleb cradled the deer's head in his hands I wept harder than I ever had. For here it was, waiting for me all along: death, inescapable death, everywhere. Always.

fourteen

THE NEXT MORNING, THE MEMORY OF THE KILL RUSHED
into my thoughts before I could raise my head from the
mattress. The boys had been waiting for the deer to arrive,
and had carried it into the dugout, roping its limbs to a
broken branch. I retreated to the cavern quickly, back to
a sleeping Arden. I couldn't stand to see it opened up and
the skin peeled back, the tender meat exposed.

I turned on the lantern by our bedside, filling the room
with a soft white glow. Caleb had brought us a pile of
clothes, freshly washed in the lake. I stood and pulled on
a button-down shirt. I still didn't know where the owner
of the children's books was, or why he'd abandoned his

room. On the side of the desk sat a notepad. I pulled it out, taking in the four simple words: *My name is Paul.* The handwriting was wobbly, the letters unevenly spaced. I thought of what Caleb had said about the boys, how in some ways they'd had it worse than the girls. I closed my eyes and imagined Ruby being herded into that room with the narrow beds. I heard her question the doctors, in the innocent way only she could. *Where are our books? When is our first trip to the City of Sand? Why are we being strapped down?* They had taken so much from us, but we'd been given one thing at least. I would always know how to read, to write, to spell my own name.

Behind me, bare feet smacked against the mud floor. I turned just in time to see a tiny person dart toward me and yank the notepad right out of my hand. The boy had matted, light brown hair and wore mud-caked overalls with no T-shirt underneath.

"Where did you come from?" I asked softly, not wanting to scare him. "Who are you?"

"This is my brother's." He held up the pad like a prize.

"I wasn't trying to pry," I said slowly, not taking my gaze off his small body. I remembered the little girls who were in School—a year behind us, then two years after, then three, the classes shrinking down to nothing as the

King organized people in the City, sorting the orphans out. Some children were occasionally found in the woods, born to Strays in the wake of the plague, but it was rare. I hadn't seen a child this young in so long. And I couldn't remember ever having seen a male child. "I just—"

"He was learning to read," the boy said. His toe touched down on the floor, punting a pebble across the dirt. He looked no more than six and had the expression of someone who rarely smiled. "He was going to teach me, but then he died."

I glanced in the corner, where Arden lay motionless on the mattress, her skin gleaming with sweat. A full plate of vegetables sat at her side from the night before. "What was wrong with him? Was he sick?" The words caught in my throat as I watched her face.

"He'd just started hunting. Caleb said it was a flash flood." He flipped through the notepad as he spoke, revealing pages and pages of shaky scribbles. "Paul took care of me when our parents disappeared. He was the one who brought me here."

"I'm sorry," I said.

"I don't get why everyone says that." When he looked up at me his eyes caught the light. "It's not like it's your fault."

"I guess . . ." I thought of the visions that came to me every time I was pulled into sleep. Pip in a thin white bed, her stomach protruding over her legs. Sometimes she was wriggling from the restraints' leather grip, screaming out to the others who lay beside her, reaching for hands she could not hold. Other times she'd be as I remembered her, at her desk doing math problems, her pencil banging out a familiar, steady beat on the wood. She'd turn suddenly, her face flooded with anger as she exposed the pregnant mound of her profile. *Why is this happening?* she'd ask, taking a step toward me, then another. *Why?* I'd keep saying the same words—*I'm so sorry, I'm so sorry*—until she lunged at me and I'd wake up.

I cleared my throat and met the boy's eyes. ". . . Sometimes it's like saying *I'm sad*. Or *I'm hurting for you*. Maybe it's silly. Maybe it's just what people say."

The boy studied me, taking in the hair that fell past my shoulders, the ends frayed. I'd combed it with my fingers to keep it from tangling into knots. "They told me you're a girl," he said.

I nodded.

"Are you my mother?"

"No," I said, "I'm not."

Silence followed. He picked at the chapped skin on his lips for a moment.

"I'm Benny," he finally said as he shuffled to the door. "Want to see my room? You can meet my bunkmate, Silas."

I hesitated. My gaze moved to Arden. She was curled up, her eyes squeezed shut as they had been since yesterday evening. "All right," I said to the little boy, glad to have someone to talk to. "Let's go."

I followed him down the winding corridors to a small, narrow room. Two mattresses sat on the floor and mud-covered trucks and cans were scattered across the dirt. Another boy with chestnut skin was drawing in the hard ground with a stick. His black hair was all different lengths, revealing patches of scalp, and he wore a long T-shirt tucked into a familiar accessory—a purple tutu.

So this was Silas. The little girl I'd chased through the forest was in fact a little boy.

"I know you," I said, stepping toward him. "You frightened me that night. Why wouldn't you stop running when I called?"

Silas froze in my gaze. "I was running," he said, dropping the stick on the floor, "because you were chasing me." His feet were folded beneath him, making him look even smaller than he was.

"Are there more of you?" I asked. Silas picked up his stick and carved more circles in the dirt. He ignored me, instead focusing on his drawings. "You're the youngest?"

Benny plopped down beside him. He turned and for the first time I noticed a long, pink scar stretching from the back of his neck to his ear, half hidden by his matted hair. "Yup. Then there's Huxley. He's eleven. He plays with us sometimes, but everybody else is always doing chores or in training."

"Training for what?"

Silas kept his gaze to the floor. He drew something that looked like a deer, making Xs for the horns.

"The older boys become hunters when they turn fifteen," Benny answered.

"So your brother was fifteen," I said. I'd assumed Paul was a child, because of all the picture books. But he must have started with the simplest things he could find. "And he was teaching himself to read?"

Benny nodded. "Do you know how to read?" he asked.

"I do," I said.

"Will you teach me?"

"Yes," I said, "I will."

For the first time since I'd met him, Benny smiled, revealing a missing front tooth. With a sudden inspiration I grabbed Silas's stick and kneeled on the floor. I scratched the word quickly, without thinking, into the hard earth. Then, in one swift motion, I underlined it. "Do you know what that is?" I asked.

Silas stared at the letters and back at me, as though he was surprised that my hand had made those letters appear. He shook his head.

"That's your name," I said, pointing at the letters one by one. "S-I-L-A-S." Then I scribbled another word below it. "And this spells Benny."

Benny smiled, his one front tooth jutting out at an angle.

Silas stared at me, his mouth forming a small O. "Silas," he repeated, pressing his fingers to the ground.

I set the stick down and stood, flushed with pleasure. "Wait here, for just a minute," I said, thinking of all those books that sat, unread, on Paul's old desk. "I'll be right back."

———

BENNY STOOD IN FRONT OF THE MUD WALL, SCRATCHING out the letters with a stick. "Yes, that's right," I said, as the room of boys watched in silence. He finished the Y and stood back, spelling out the word in block letters.

"Benny," he read, his face exploding in a toothless grin.

"Very good," I said, taking the stack of children's books off the table. What started as the two little boys etching their letters in the ground had grown as a few of the older boys had poked their heads into the room and taken seats.

"Let's read a book," I said, pulling one off the top of the pile. When I had retrieved them, I was delighted to recognize a few from School. "Once there was a tree," I read, showing the pages around so everyone could see. "And she loved a little boy. And every day the boy would come—" I paused. Silas's hand was raised. It was the very first thing I'd taught them, after I began the lesson and they all tried to shout over one another.

"What do you mean she loved him? What is that?" he asked.

Kevin, the boy with the cracked glasses, let out an annoyed sigh. "It means he wants to kiss a girl. It's what happened before the plague." He smiled up at me, a pink-cheeked, bashful smile.

"Kiss a girl?" Silas asked incredulously.

Huxley perked up. "No, it's not that. This is a tree. The tree isn't kissing the boy."

"What are you guys talking about," Silas asked, twisting his face in confusion.

"You can love anyone," I interrupted, looking around at the group. "Love is just"—I searched for the right words—"caring about someone very deeply. Feeling like that person matters to you, like your whole world would be sadder without them in it." I thought about Pip's staccato laugh, or jumping from bed to bed with Ruby, the way we always did Saturday mornings, when we were waiting for our showers.

After a long pause, Benny glanced up. "I loved my brother," he said.

"I loved my mother," a fifteen-year-old named Michael added.

"I loved my mother, too," I said. "I still do. That's the thing—it never goes away, even if the person does." I waited a moment, then opened the book again. "So every day the boy would come and gather her leaves and make them into a crown—"

"Kevin! Michael! Aaron! Where are you?" Leif's voice boomed down the hall. He turned the corner, his muscular body streaked with ash and mud. Those black, marble eyes stared at me again, not betraying any feeling. "Where are the buckets?"

A few of the older boys sprang up from the floor. "We were going to do it after . . . after we finish the book."

"The *book*?" Leif asked, stalking toward them. He did not look at me, kept his head turned, as though I were the table, a chair, the floor beneath his feet. "You will do it now, because you were supposed to do it this morning. I want all the buckets of rainwater inside, around the fire."

"Can't it wait a few minutes? We're almost done," I said before I could stop myself.

The boys turned, surprised at the sound of my voice.

Leif stepped toward me, his musky smell filling the space between us. "Wait for what?" He snatched the book from my hand. "This? These boys don't need to be reading children's books. They need to learn to fend for themselves."

"And they'll be able to." I straightened up. "But they also should be able to understand a basic road sign, or how to write their own name."

Leif looked around at the class, nearly a dozen of them packed tightly together in the small space. His mouth opened and closed slowly, like a fish washed onshore, struggling to breathe. Then he met eyes with Kevin, the oldest in the room, and nodded.

"You can fill the buckets immediately after your lesson. As for you . . ." He looked at me. Despite his cold gaze I could've sworn I noticed a lightness in his expression, a soft give around his lips, the closest thing I'd ever seen to a smile. "If you're going to stay here and teach these boys then you should know what they're about. The older ones"—he pointed with his thick finger to Kevin and Aaron, who were cooling their backs on the mud wall—"will be leaving the dugout soon, on hunting and guard duty. The initiation ceremony begins the day after next, at sundown." He went out the door, stooping so his head didn't hit the dip in the ceiling.

I looked back at the class, the book still in my hands. I could feel the shifting of power, as real as if the earth beneath me had changed. Energy surged through my body and I spoke the words, the cavern seeming bigger now. "And every day the boy would come and gather her leaves . . ."

fifteen

LATER THAT NIGHT, WHEN ARDEN'S CHOKED COUGHS
had given way to the rhythmic breaths of sleep, I grabbed
the flashlight from its nest in the floor and started back
into the tunnels. The camp was quiet. The twisting corridor was empty. After a few days there, I understood
the basic underground structure, the five pathways that
came out of that circular main room, creating a starlike
formation beneath the massive hill. I turned and made
my way down the second tunnel, counting the doorways
in the dark.

I kept thinking of Benny's brother, Paul, who had sat
at that desk in the corner practicing his letters, who had

stretched out on the same mattress as I had, studying the cracks in the mud ceiling. Maybe the day that he'd died, he had sensed it, like an oncoming storm. Or maybe he had slung his bow over his shoulder as he did every morning and taken off for the hunt. Maybe he had passed by Benny's room, not wanting to wake him, not knowing it was the last time—until he was locked in the tumult of the wave, churning in the white water, pulling the river into his lungs.

The sound of snoring filled the dimly lit hallway as I crept forward, running my hand along the stones in the wall. I still had so many questions. What had happened in the camps beyond the work, the hauling of bricks and stones? How did children as young as Benny and Silas get into camp? It wasn't enough to have passing details. I was awake with the same desire that had often overtaken me at School. Headmistress once called it "the thirst for knowledge."

I turned a corner at the sixth doorway and he was before me, in his wrinkled shirt and ripped shorts. His legs were draped over one arm of a deep, cushioned chair, his head draped over the other.

"Caleb?" I asked. "Are you asleep?"

He startled awake, looking around quickly as if

to remember where he was. Then he rubbed his face, smoothed back his hair and smiled.

"Welcome to my humble abode." He gestured to the bare mattress on the floor, covered only with a comforter, its feathers sprouting up from the seams. On the table beside it was a metal radio and handset like the ones I'd seen at School. Maps were tacked up on the wall, their edges curled from the moisture.

"What are you doing with all these books?" I asked, stepping toward a tall stack on the floor. I ran my fingers down the spines, recognizing a few familiar titles from School: *Heart of Darkness, The Great Gatsby,* and *To the Lighthouse.*

Caleb came beside me, his warm shoulder brushing against mine. "I do this funny thing sometimes," he said, shooting me a mischievous grin. "I open a book, and I look at each page. It's called reading."

"I know what reading is!" I laughed. Heat crept up my neck and face, settling in my cheeks. I ran my fingers through my hair. I hadn't seen a mirror since School. "But how? Benny said no one had learned to read here."

"You met Benny, then?" Caleb asked. His eyes seemed to be searching my face, scanning my lips and brows and cheeks.

I nodded. "Earlier today. And Silas and some of the other boys, too. Silas was the little girl I thought I saw. He was wearing that tutu."

Caleb laughed. "He found that tutu in boxes we'd raided from a warehouse. Leif and some of the older boys knew what it was, but how can we tell him? He loves it too much."

I smiled, my nerves suddenly awake in my body. I picked up *Heart of Darkness*, thankful to have its weight in my hands, steadying my trembling fingers. "I started to teach them to read. You never showed them the alphabet? Their names?"

"I went into the labor camps when I was seven, so I had learned a bit before the plague. My mother had taught me some basic things before she died—smaller words and the sounds. And then after, here, I would read at night to . . ." He stared at the ceiling. The stubble on his face was getting thicker, creating dark shadows along his chin and neck. ". . . to escape, I guess. It was never an option, teaching the boys, especially not with Leif around. As the oldest, we need to hunt, fish, survey the land, and keep watch for troops in the area. All day, every day. They need food more than they need books. Unfortunately." He sighed and met my eyes. "I'm glad you're teaching them, though."

He held my gaze until I finally had to look away. "*You read all of these?*" I glanced at *Anna Karenina* and *On the Road*, which looked strange sandwiched between *Art History for Dummies* and *The Complete Book of Swimming*.

"Every word." Caleb laughed. "I'm not such a caveman after all, huh?"

Caleb's long tattered gray shirt was unbuttoned, revealing the occasional glimpse of his tanned chest. "I didn't really say that, did I?"

"You didn't have to," he replied.

I crossed the room to another pile and Caleb followed, his steps right behind mine, as though shadowing me in a dance. "I was wrong," I said. Standing so close to him I could see the specks of brown in his pale green irises.

Caleb circled me, laughing, as if I were some delightful creature he'd discovered in the brush. "Oh really?" was all he said.

"Oh, this one . . ." I picked up *To the Lighthouse*. Its pages were curled up at the corners. "Charles Tansley! What a nightmare. Who is he to say women can't paint, women can't write? And the way Mr. Ramsay just forgets about his wife after she died—he's practically swooning over Lily at the end!"

Caleb tilted his head. "I assumed your education was skewed, but I never realized how much."

"What do you mean?" I asked.

Caleb took a step closer and I could smell the smoke on his skin. "Mr. Ramsay is in mourning, he's devastated. That's why he takes James to the lighthouse—he's still thinking of that argument he had with his wife years ago." I furrowed my brow, trying to process what Caleb said. "The book shows what happens without Mrs. Ramsay, how important a mother is, how quickly everything fell apart without her," he continued. "They all loved her."

I remembered the lesson at School, with Teacher Agnes lecturing about men's desire for younger women, or the inability of men to fulfill the emotional needs of the people around them. It all seemed so clear then.

"That's just your opinion," I tried, shaking my head.

But Caleb didn't look away. His face was half lit by the glow of the lantern, making his features softer. "That's what happens in the book, Eve." He rapped on its hard cover.

I dropped the book and sat down on the armchair, for the first time not minding the musty smell that seemed inescapable at the camp.

"It's just—" I said, feeling the sudden swell of

embarrassment. I thought of that night in the doctor's office, right before I left School. Teacher Florence had told me the King wanted to repopulate the earth efficiently, without all the complications of families, marriage, and love. She had said the girls had done it willingly at first. It made some sick sense. They must've thought if we feared men we would never desire them. We would never want love, or families of our own. Then we would be more willing to do whatever they asked of us. "That's not how I learned it."

I turned away, hoping Caleb didn't see my eyes, washed over by emotion. I had worked so hard at School, taken detailed notes on each lesson, scribbling down the margins until my fingers cramped. And for what? To fill my head with lies?

"Sometimes it seems like all the things I need to know, I don't. And all the things I do know are completely wrong." I dug my fingernails into my palm, suddenly frustrated. Anger swelled inside me. I started to the door but Caleb grabbed my hand, pulling me back.

"Wait." He curled my fingers around his, just for a moment, before dropping them. "What do you mean?"

"Twelve years in School and I . . . I don't even know how to swim," I managed, remembering the panic I felt that night at the river. I couldn't hunt or fish, I didn't even know where in the world I *was*. I was completely useless.

He stood, walking me to the doorway. "Here, Eve," he said as he grabbed his copy of *To the Lighthouse* off the floor. "Have my book. You could read it again—for yourself."

We stayed in the mud threshold for a moment, his head just grazing the ceiling. I ran my fingers over the broken cover, considering what he'd said. Maybe here, in this dugout, away from Teacher and the lectures, the book would be different. Maybe *I'd* be different. I listened to our breaths, now in sync.

"This still doesn't solve my swimming problem," I said. I couldn't keep from smiling as I met Caleb's gaze.

"That's the easy part." He rested his hand on the wall, inches above my head. Short, blunt stubble spread out over his chin, glittering in the light of the lantern. "I can show you how to swim in a day."

"One day?" I asked, wondering if he could hear the banging of my heart. "I don't believe it."

"Believe it," he said. He leveled his pale green eyes at me again. We were in a contest to see who would look away first. *One*, I counted in my head. *Two, three . . .*

I broke, finally, ducking under his arm and into the

tunnel. "Well then it's a plan," I said, starting back toward my room. When I spun around, his eyes were still locked on me. "Good night," I called over my shoulder, feeling the warmth of his gaze as I walked down the dank, musty hall and settled back in my bed.

sixteen

WHEN WE REACHED THE SHORE CALEB PEELED OFF HIS
T-shirt and dove into the lake, his legs together, kicking
just beneath its sparkling surface. He shot out into the
deeper water until he disappeared under the inky black.

I waited. A minute passed. Then another. I scanned
the wide expanse of blue but he was nowhere to be seen.
"Caleb?" I called out. I took off down the shore, searching for any sign of him, but the lake was eerily still.

Finally he broke the surface, almost a hundred yards
away, the water splashing white around his head. I let out
a deep breath, gasping with him, as though I'd been holding my breath.

"Show off!" I yelled.

I dropped the pilled towel from my shoulders, revealing the "bathing suit" I'd put together to swim: a pair of jean shorts under my beaten School jumper—the fabric ripped where the crest used to be. I'd cut it off that morning with a knife, thinking of Pip.

I dipped my toes in and my pulse quickened. The water was cold. The sun was dropping below the trees, the air more biting than usual. I felt dizzy as I stared into the spot where the lake grew deeper and darker. I let the smooth stones massage the soles of my feet and tried to work up my nerves. I was feeling more comfortable, more confident, brave even. Arden had shown improvement; she remained in bed, but she was drinking more and eating more, and the color was returning to her face. I didn't wince when I passed Leif in the corridor anymore, and I was no longer afraid to explore the camp. Slowly, surely, I was easing into our temporary home.

Caleb swam back, his muscular body turning side to side as each arm came up before plunging back into the deep. When he reached the shallow water, he threw his head back. "Now is as good a time as any," he said, gesturing with one hand. "It's not deep here."

The water was only up to his waist. But I thought of

that night at School, of the choking feeling as the ground slipped out from beneath me. I moved forward slowly, carefully, letting the cold lake cover me inch by inch. Caleb came forward and offered me his hand.

I took it without thinking, feeling the same heat I'd felt in his room. My skin buzzed from the closeness.

"See?" He smiled, as the water beaded on his tanned, freckled chest. "It's not so bad."

After a few steps the lake rose to my waist. I looked down, startled by the sudden disappearance of my feet. I wanted to go back, to return to the shore and stand on certain ground. But Caleb grabbed my other hand and stared at me, his pale green eyes demanding that I meet them. We walked together into the deep.

"Are you okay?" Caleb asked when the water was up to my shoulders. I nodded, waiting for my heart to slow. "All right then. Now we'll dunk. One, two—"

"Wait!" I yelled. "You want me to go under?" I needed more time—to adjust to the temperature, to prepare.

"Yes. Let's stay under for as long as you can. On three." I was about to protest, but Caleb started the count again. "One, two, three," he said, and I took in air, my lips pressing closed as we slipped below the surface.

I was completely submerged, my heart pounding in my

ears. I could hear my lungs as they let out air, the bubbles floating up to the sky, leaving me below in the cool water. Caleb was two feet in front of me, eyes open, hands in mine. His face was so soft, so earnest and sweet that I forgot, if only for an instant, that we were different. That he was of the other sex, the one I had been warned about. The one I had spent my life fearing.

Right then he was just Caleb. I smiled and he smiled, our arms forming a circle in the stillness of the water.

———————

WE STAYED OUT UNTIL THE SKY DIMMED. I PRACTICED holding my breath, dunking under repeatedly until I didn't flinch when the lake swallowed me. Caleb taught me how to tread water and kick forward beneath the surface. He showed me how to float, his fingers resting on the small of my back as I filled my stomach with air. I closed my eyes, trying to pretend that my pale legs weren't exposed, that the wet jumper wasn't clinging to the curves of my body.

The sky was turning from purple to gray as we walked back through the woods, the dried pine needles break-ing beneath our feet. I wrapped the towel around my shoulders, but I couldn't stop shivering. Caleb took off his sweatshirt and offered it to me, rolling up the sleeves for me to stick my hands through.

"I finished the book. I stayed up all night reading it," I said as I pulled the thick, soft material down around me. It still held some of his body heat and I felt warmer already. "You were right. It's not quite the story I was told."

"I thought it might be better a second time." Water dripped from his dreadlocks down his back, winding around the ropy muscles of his shoulders.

"I've been wondering . . ." I started. "How did you learn so much about the world outside the labor camps?" I asked. "How did you get here? How did you know where to go? Tell me everything."

Caleb waited for me to catch up. We started through a narrow path, ducking under low tree limbs. He walked in front of me, pushing branches up so I could slip beneath them, then getting ahead of me so he could do it again.

"Those weeks after Asher died were strange," he said, keeping his eyes on the trail. "Leif refused to work, and was in solitary confinement most nights. All the other boys were scared to do anything that would anger the guards. The one thing we were allowed at the labor camps were these black metal radios, and the boys would all lay out on their bunks listening to the broadcast from the City of Sand."

"I've heard some of those broadcasts, too, at School," I said, ringing water out of my long hair. Once a month we would sit in the auditorium and listen to the stories of what was happening in the City. The King would tell of the giant skyscrapers that were being built or the new Schools that were opening up for children inside the City's walls. He was building in the desert—*something from nothing*, as he said—and the City would be surrounded by walls so high everyone would be protected. From rebels, from disease, from the dangers of the world. At the time, I'd found comfort in his words. "The King made it sound so noble, so exciting."

Caleb kicked a pebble with his bare feet. "I remember that voice. I'll remember it forever." Caleb punted the rock into the woods, his expression turning darker. His skin flushed red. "He never mentioned the orphans who worked in the City. How boys as young as seven were disassembling buildings for fourteen hours a day in one hundred and ten degree heat. How some were crushed by collapsing walls or fell from the skyscrapers. Or the girls who were being used as broodmares. He made it sound like The New America was for everyone, that we would all be included, but it was built on the backs of the orphans. The only place for us was under their feet."

As we walked I let my hands graze the tall grass that grew alongside the trail. "So who is raising the children? The survivors in the City?"

"Right now they're sitting in their new houses that overlook the canals that fourteen-year-old boys dredged up, and they're feeding their babies that eighteen-year-old girls gave birth to, or they're skiing on their indoor ski slopes and eating at the restaurants at the tops of sky-scrapers where orphans work for free. It's disgusting." He grimaced.

"How did you escape?" I asked again. I thought of the horrors of that labor camp, of Asher alone in the wild with his legs pinned down, or boys as small as Silas car-rying stones on their backs.

"It happened one night after a particularly infuriating speech about the new royal palace," Caleb began, as he extended a hand back to me, helping me over a boulder. "I couldn't sleep. I kept staring at Asher and Leif's empty bunk. The guards had found a two-year-old boy in the woods. He was newly orphaned, and he was sobbing. It wasn't only the plague that made orphans." Caleb paused to explain: "Living conditions were so difficult after, the world in such chaos, that many children lost their parents even after the disease had passed. I had grown so numb I just listened to him crying for two hours. A gang had shot his mother. I didn't care. I was hollow. It couldn't touch me because there was nothing in me to touch. I was so . . ." Caleb stopped on the path and turned to me. He cleared his voice, careful with his words. ". . . I was so callous. I'm still embarrassed." I couldn't imagine him being so cold, not after the way he'd cradled the deer's head in his hands, stroking the soft fur on its neck until it died.

Caleb grabbed a branch, rubbing his fingers over the rough bark. "I started thinking about everything and I knew I couldn't live there much longer. It wasn't living, it wasn't a life. I was terrified and desperate. And I had the radio in my hand and I was turning it, just fiddling with it." He let out a deep breath. His fingers stopped moving. "Then I heard a voice. It was talking absolute nonsense."

"What was it saying?" I asked, stepping forward to close the space between us.

"I'll always remember that first sentence. It said, 'He especially loved people, is so happy, especially remembering Eloise.'"

I leaned in, as if getting closer to him would help me

decipher the meaning. "Who's Eloise? I don't understand." A gust of wind came through the mountains, making the trees lean. Shadows moved across Caleb's face.

"I wasn't sure at first either. The man just kept on like that. He said that a few times, and then other cryptic sentences. Always repeating the words in this haunting voice. I kept looking around wondering if I had split from reality, if I had drifted off into a dream or something. And then after the tenth time he repeated himself I stopped trying to understand the sentence and started listening to the way he said it. He was trying to tell me something, the tone in his voice was almost pleading." Caleb looked up, his eyes meeting mine. They were red and wet. "He especially loved people, is so happy, especially remembering Eloise. He especially—"

"H," I interrupted, feeling my throat tighten with emotion. "E-L-P I-S H-E-R-E."

Caleb smiled, and I felt the rest of the world fall away—the trees, the path, the mountains, the sky— leaving only us.

"Yes." He nodded. "Help is here." He reached out his hand and I pressed it between mine. "The voice kept on. Over the next few nights he revealed a place in the wild where, if you could escape, he would meet you. It took a few months, and I waited for Leif to return to make a plan together. We studied the guard's routines and found a loophole. We left one night—just the three of us."

"Three of you?"

Caleb looked at our hands, together, smiling slightly as though the sight pleased him. "We brought the little boy whose mother was shot. Silas." Caleb's fingers threaded through mine, squeezing tight as we started back up the path.

"And you came here," I said, keeping my eyes on his as we approached the clearing beyond the dugout.

"That was five years ago. The camp was already being built by a small group of boys, led by the man whose voice I heard all those nights. Moss. He started the Trail. There are safe havens all along the west, all leading to dugouts like this. Leif, Silas, and I traveled for two months to get here, sleeping in rebel houses. People are still out there, living outside of the City. They don't believe in what the King is doing either, and they help girls and boys escape."

He grabbed a log on the side of the hill and pulled, exposing the hidden door. Inside the camp was quiet and dark. I was steadied by the sound of our bare feet on the floor, walking in time.

"So that's what Teacher was talking about. Califia—

that place where Arden and I will go. On the water."
I watched Caleb as I said it, expecting a flinch—a
grimace—something that would reveal his feelings about
me leaving, but his expression betrayed nothing. Now
that Arden was able to walk, even if it was just around
our tiny room, it would only be a week or two before we'd
be gone. I wondered if I would be able to go, to just leave
the dugout and head west as I'd planned. Caleb was right
beside me, and I missed him already.

"Yes, it's another safe haven for orphans and Strays—
the biggest," was all he said.

"And Moss?" I asked. "Where is he now?"

Caleb led me through the dim tunnel. "There were
murmurings that he was inside the City, but nothing is
certain. For the most part he keeps his location secret and
he's moving around the Trail so much it's impossible to
track him. He's still sending out messages, but we haven't
seen him in over a year."

I wished I had known about the radio communications
and the Trail before I'd left School. Before I'd walked
out of our room, leaving Ruby and Pip in those narrow
beds, in their last pleasant sleep. Maybe there would be
a chance to send them word from Califia. A chance to
reach them.

I felt the soft give of Caleb's hand as we reached my doorway, the sweet smell of sweat and smoke on his skin. I noticed the freckles that spread out over his nose and forehead, where his skin was browned by the sun. Neither of us spoke. Instead I just ran my hand over his, circling my fingers over the knuckles and his nails, for once not minding that they were caked with dirt. He rested his chin on the top of my head and I breathed in, aware of the mere inch that stretched between my nose and his chest.

"You did great today," Caleb said after a long while. He squeezed my hand in good-bye.

"Thanks again for teaching me." I strode into my room, but I couldn't stop myself. I turned back. He was still standing there, filling up the doorway.

I had listened to what Teacher Agnes had said. I learned about the Illusion of Connection and the Dangers of Boys and Men, and read through the Subtle Manipulations. But beneath all that, somewhere inside me, there was a deeper knowledge. It held a place that even fear and a carefully crafted education could not touch. It was the way Caleb had sung out of tune that day in the woods—just threw his head back and sang, his voice echoing through the trees. It was the food that was set out for us every morning and every evening, the awkwardly folded towels and shirts, the bathwater he dragged in for Arden, without anyone ever having asked.

I knew, perhaps with more certainty than I knew anything else, that this was a good man.

"Good night, Eve," he said. He lowered his eyes, almost bashfully, and then disappeared into the dark.

 seventeen

"I BET AARON SWIMS THE FASTEST," BENNY SAID, SQUEEZ-
ing my hand. "He's like a fish."

We stood together on a landing just north of the dugout,
our eyes scanning the lake for any signs of the new Hunters.
Arden's fever had broken and the color in her cheeks had
returned. Her legs were still weak but she'd insisted on join-
ing and I was glad to have her there, by my side.

Arden squirmed free of Silas's tiny hand. "Your skin
is sweaty," she told him, wiping her palm on her frayed
denim shorts. "It's like holding a slug." She wiped it again
and again, her pale nose scrunched in disgust. "What?"
she asked me. "What's so funny?"

"You really are feeling better." I laughed. She had been out of bed for less than an hour and her patience was already ground down to nothing. I took that as a good sign.

All day, while I was inside teaching the remaining boys, Caleb and Leif had searched the woods for troops. When the area was declared safe they rode the new Hunters to the other side of the lake, where they began their arduous trek. The new Hunters were to run ten miles around the rocky shore, plummeting finally into the cool depths of the water. Now, at any moment, they would swim around the tree line and run up the beach to where four spears waited for them, their stone blades bone-white in the last of the day's sun.

I watched that spot onshore where the trees leaned over the water, the spot where Caleb had taught me to swim. Last night, I dreamed that we were in the lake again, the water holding us, his hands in mine. All day, as I walked Arden around the dugout or corrected the words Benny spelled in the mud, he filled my thoughts. His smile, his fingers touching the small of my back, the smell of his skin on my sweatshirt . . .

Kyler, a tall boy with orange curls, ran toward the cliff's edge. "There they are! I see them!" he cried. He was holding cracked binoculars, and Benny and Silas jumped up, trying to grab them, desperate to look. There, where the water kissed the sky, was a moving speck.

Soon after, the boys came into sight beyond the trees, their bodies heaving in and out of the water like great leaping fish. Michael was out front, his Afro visible even from the rocky landing.

"They're superfast!" Silas said. His face paint had smeared, leaving golden streaks on his hands. "Look at Aaron go!"

"Go, go, go!" Benny cheered. The crowd behind us sprinted to the cliff, bathed in the pink glow of the setting sun. A few of the twelve-year-old boys banged sticks together in unison, making a *whack! whack! whack!* sound that grew louder and louder.

As the boys neared the shore, a beaten-up canoe rounded the trees behind them, with Leif and Caleb each paddling on one side. The oldest boys of the camp followed in four more boats. Their faces were painted black, with lines across their cheeks and down the bridge of their noses. Seeing Caleb, his arms straining against the current, my body swelled with a passing joy.

Of all the things Teacher Agnes had misinterpreted, I only recognized one thing as being wrong at the time.

Happiness is the anticipation of future happiness, she'd explained, as she held a copy of *Great Expectations* in her hands. I remembered then the day Ruby had found a kitten in the bushes, how we took turns rubbing the soft fur of its belly or letting it curl up in our laps. I remembered how we'd stacked our mattresses after Headmistress had gone to sleep, the tower high above Pip's bed. I knew that feeling of jumping, the give of the springs under my feet, the way my body tumbled off, loose with laughter. *No,* I thought then, and now, watching as Caleb glanced up at me and smiled that kind, brilliant smile. *Happiness is a moment.*

Aaron hit the shallows of the lake, running with the water splashing around his knees. Michael followed, then Charlie, and finally Kevin. Kevin squinted into the sun, his steps tentative without his glasses. They darted over some bleached tree limbs to where four spears were standing, their ends plunged into the sand.

"Look at them go!" Silas cried, gripping his tutu.

Michael reached his spear first, launching it into the air. One by one the spears all flew and the new Hunters doubled over from exhaustion. Silas and Benny ran from our sides and followed the younger boys down through the trail ledge, where they greeted Aaron, Kevin, Michael, and Charlie.

Leif and Caleb's canoe landed onshore, its bottom scraping against the rocks. They made their way through the crowd, past the excited boys, to where the new Hunters were. Caleb caught my eye, offering me the slightest smile. *Hi,* I mouthed.

"Your ears are turning red." Arden nudged me in the side. "Get it together, Eve." I reached for my hair, pulling the dark brown strands around the sides of my face.

Leif summoned the four new Hunters forward to stand in front of him in a line. His shoulders were the color of bricks from being outside, on the water, rowing for so long.

"Today you've proved yourselves as men, and tomorrow you'll be ready to go out on your own to hunt. Much is expected from you. These boys"—Leif gestured to younger ones around us, to Benny, whose nose was now running—"need protection, leaders to ensure they are safe here, away from the labor camps. These woods are your home now, these boys are your family. We are brothers." At these words, the boys rested their fingers against the circular crests tattooed on their shoulders.

Caleb pulled a piece of coal from his shorts pocket. "It is time for you to swear allegiance to the Trail. Do you promise to use your skills for the good of the orphans, both free and enslaved?"

The boys all nodded. "I do," they said in unison.

Caleb stepped forward, running his thumb across Michael's forehead and down the bridge of his nose. Caleb kept moving down the row, adding the marks to Charlie's face, then Aaron's, then Kevin's.

"You are Hunters now. You are men!" Leif boomed. He raised his arms in the air, fists balled, the muscles straining against the skin. He looked like those statues I'd seen in my art books, the ones by Michelangelo, chiseled from stone.

Silas was the first to break from the pack. He ran for Kevin and grabbed his side, nearly tackling him in a hug. The other boys darted forward, hooting and cheering, clapping the new Hunters on the back. Michael lifted Benny onto his shoulders as Aaron thanked Leif and Caleb again, his hand squeezing theirs tight.

When the excited yelps subsided, the new Hunters congregated around a few tree stumps, where heaping plates of boar meat, jugs of water, and bowls of colorful berries sat. The boys waited, their voices quieting, until Caleb spoke.

"Before we eat, we must give thanks. First that the new Hunters made it through their trials and continue to be strong protectors of the other boys. Understanding that every meal is a collaboration of souls, we thank the earth that gave us these berries; Michael, who picked them by hand; the roasted boar who surrendered his life so we may be nourished by its meat. We thank those who prepared this dinner for us with care." Caleb raised a jug in the air, his eyes meeting mine. "And we must thank our two friends who have joined us, in particular your new teacher, who has shown great thought and nurturing in each new lesson."

It took a moment, and then the sudden pressure of Arden's fingers burying into my arm, to understand he was speaking about me. My throat tightened. *He had noticed.* Perhaps he had stopped there, in the doorway of Benny's room, looking at the books piled on the table or the plastic toys that had been cleared from the floors so the students could sit. He had been watching.

"To Arden and Eve," Leif added, as he grabbed another jug from the tree stump and raised it in the air. He kept his brooding eyes down, not looking at us. The other boys turned, all of them to give thanks—some with a nod, others with a smile—before passing the jug around and taking long, slow sips. Then the seriousness lifted and the boys dug into the spread of roasted boar, berries, and wild turkey.

Finally, when the new Hunters had consumed enough and their feverishness subsided, Leif spoke again. "Tonight is the full moon," he said, pointing above him. It was just appearing, its faint outline clearer as the pink sky deepened to purple. "And we've discovered that the troops have changed their direction. They've abandoned the southern outpost. Which means tonight—"

"Raid!" Michael yelled, bits of boar flying from his fingers as he raised his hands. "We'll raid their supplies!"

Silas broke into a sudden cheer. "Candy! Candy! Candy!"

"Yes." Leif nodded, a slight smile on his lips. His thick bun had come undone, sending his damp black curls cascading over his shoulders. "The time is right for a raid. We'll meet back here in an hour."

The crowd of boys started toward the dugout, carrying the last of the feast. I felt an arm wrap around my bare shoulder. "May I?" Caleb asked.

My arm tingled where our skin met. We walked together, my steps matching his. Could he sense my thoughts about him? Did he know that he'd worked his way into my dreams, where I missed him, even in sleep?

"Yes," was all I could manage. "Yes."

eighteen

"I SAW YOU SNUGGLING UP WITH CALEB." ARDEN WAS already in our cave when I returned, bundled in a jacket, her legs folded on the mattress. She held the flashlight to her face, then turned it on me for a response.

I ignored her, instead pulling on a pilled sweater for warmth. The night air was stiff with a chill and I wasn't sure how far the outpost was.

"Headmistress Burns would not approve," she pressed.

I covered the beam with my hand. "Oh stop," was all I could say.

"Don't 'Oh stop' me." Arden laughed. She gestured with the flashlight. The beam moved over her blunt bob and a sliver of milky white leg, settling on her pale face. "I'm sick for a week and you're practically falling in—" Her hand covered her mouth. I thought she was going to cough, but she stayed quiet.

"What is it, Arden?"

She nodded behind me, to where Caleb stood in the doorway, clad in a thick brown jacket and knit cap, his hair tucked up inside it.

"You're falling into this teaching routine . . ." Arden tried, but even I was not convinced. She stood, awkwardly pushing past Caleb into the hall. "I'll meet you two by the fire," she said, before disappearing into the tunnel.

I turned away from him, pulling on another thick sweater. "So are we riding with you?" I asked, trying to hammer the nerves out of my voice. "Arden is feeling better. She swears she's well enough to go."

Caleb grabbed my hand. Then he looked down, as if considering my slender fingers laced with his. "It's not that. When Leif said the troops abandoned the outpost . . ." he began. "It's because they're moving north, toward the road."

"It's because of me, isn't it," I said, before Caleb could go on. It was half-question, half-statement, but Caleb's silence confirmed what I already knew. "They changed their direction because of me." I closed my eyes, but all I saw were the headlights of their Jeeps shining on the road, looking for the girl from the flyer.

Caleb leaned closer. The charcoal lines had been rinsed from his face, leaving only the faint smell of fire. "It might not be safe for you to go on the raid tonight. An encounter with the troops is always dangerous, and it may be too much of a risk." His fingers moved through mine, wrapping my hand in his fist.

It was so easy to be afraid. Even in this underground dugout, where the troops could walk above us without knowing of our presence, my heart quickened. I wanted to curl up on the bare mattress, wrapped in a cocoon of blankets, and give up, to plant myself down here indefinitely. But this was nothing new. They would always be after me. Every flashlight over the lake was them. Every puttering engine was them. They were every shadowy figure lurking behind the trees.

My whole life had been spent in the confines of the School's walls—eating when I was told, drinking when I was told, swallowing the slick blue pills that rocked my stomach. What was one night outside? Couldn't I allow myself that?

"What if I still want to go?"

"Then you'll go," he said. "But I wanted you to know the danger."

"There's always danger." His green eyes met mine.

I was starting to see it, how it could happen—Caleb and me. Out in the wild there was no thinking, only Califia ahead of us, the swift travel that consumed the days. But underground, teaching the boys in Benny's room, leaning against the mud wall at night, after Arden had fallen asleep, I imagined staying here. I needed more time. With Caleb, with the younger boys. A stretch of weeks or months didn't feel like enough . . . I wanted more. And what if it did work out, what if it could? What then?

We could live together here—it was possible. At least until Moss had assembled enough rebels to combat the King's troops. At least until I could retrieve Pip. It would be dangerous, but we'd be careful to remain hidden. Caleb and I could build a life, however small. A life together.

"Just stay close to me and if anything happens we'll break off from the group." His gaze traced the lines of my mouth, his eyes finally settling on mine. His breath filled my ears and I smelled the charcoal again as I leaned closer. He was just inches away, those pale green eyes still looking at me, watching. I couldn't stop myself. I pressed my mouth to his. A warmth spread through my body and into my fingers as we moved into one another, his lips giving way.

In an instant, I realized what I'd done. I pulled back, my hand breaking free of his to rest on my forehead. "I'm sorry, I just—" But he pulled me closer. I rested my forehead lightly on his cheek. His fingers worked their way down my head, threading my thick brown hair between them, until they settled in the tender hollow behind my neck.

"Don't be sorry," he said. He held me in the dim cave. I wrapped my hands around his back and gripped his sides. We didn't move until the sound of voices echoed down the tunnel, calling out for the raid.

nineteen

I HELD ONTO CALEB, LETTING MYSELF RELAX INTO THE musty cushion of his jacket. Arden clutched my shoulders as we rode through the thick wood, the trees just visible through scattered starlight. She'd questioned me before we'd set off, noting the sudden pink wash over my cheeks, the way I kept bringing my fingers to my lips, touching them to confirm they were still there. She'd laughed when I'd eagerly jumped on the horse, settling into the middle spot, where my head nestled into Caleb's back. Anyone could see that things between us had changed. But I kept the news close to my chest anyway, wanting it to exist a little longer, just mine, to have and to wonder over.

In front of us, Leif steered his horses around boulders and in between fallen tree branches on the way to the southern outpost. The horses pounded the dirt, their hooves keeping a steady beat. We made our way around the rocky shore of the lake, its slick, inky surface mirroring the moon. "It's only a little farther," Caleb whispered. A hawk swooped down in front of us, cutting a path across the sky.

A gun fired miles off, echoing through the mountains. Arden pulled me tighter, her fingers digging into my skin. Ahead, Leif turned his horse into a patch of overgrown grass. Six other horses followed, black silhouettes, carrying the older boys and the four new Hunters. Silas, Benny, and the younger boys had remained in the dugout, sleeping soundly with the morning's promise of chocolate bars and sucking candies.

Leif glanced around, his face half in shadow. "The outpost is a hundred yards ahead," he whispered. "If anything happens, do not use force, no matter what."

"If anything happens?" I repeated, whispering into Caleb's ear. "What does he mean?"

"It's only a precaution," Caleb said. I could feel his heartbeat as I rested on his back. "Killing a New American soldier, even in self-defense, is an offense punishable by death." He brought the horse into a slow trot. "An incident happened at another outpost a year back. The King retaliated by executing an escaped orphan." I winced, imagining a young boy, alone and afraid, coming up against the King's troops.

We left the horses in the clearing, their necks bent as they chewed on grass. Caleb took my hand in his own and that familiar warmth returned. *I'm okay, we're okay, everything's okay.* The repetition calmed me. Beyond the trees I could make out a converted house, its facade barely visible in the moonlight that slipped between the branches. The windows were boarded up with corrugated tin, and the metal front door was chained and padlocked. Leif canvassed the building and appeared on the other side. "All clear." He nodded to Caleb.

The boys started up the wraparound porch. Michael pried at the windows with his knife, wedging it under an old shingle. Kevin picked at the padlock but couldn't unlock it.

"Let me try," Arden said, jumping down from the porch banister.

Kevin smiled up at her as she worked the pick, freeing the lock with just a few slight turns of her wrist.

"Voilà!" The door to the storeroom swung open. The

boys hooted and Aaron and Charlie wrestled each other inside. Even Leif smiled as we rushed ahead, flipping on the government generator. It was the same kind we'd had at School, the whir of it growing in those first few seconds, the lights turning on one by one, until the room swelled with a loud, steady hum.

"How'd you do that?" I asked, stunned.

"Just a little trick I learned in School." Arden shrugged playfully.

We surveyed the main floor, which had been cleared of furniture to make room for storage. Every spare space was packed with delicacies I'd never seen before: cans of pineapples, mangoes, and a meat spread called spam. Shelves were bolted to the walls of the living room, one whole row filled with gallons and gallons of water, in plastic jugs the color of the sky.

Michael rushed over to a cardboard box and pulled out white paper packages, tossing them around. "Mmmmm," he said, dumping the sugary red substance into his mouth. "Fundip."

"Dig in," Caleb called from the other side of the room. He had climbed up the side of the wooden shelves, pulling down a box of long, thin meat sticks, wrapped in yellow plastic. Aaron tucked a fistful into his jeans.

The gorging went on for over an hour, with each box, each plastic package, each carton, containing another delectable surprise. Leif passed out bags of Tootsie Rolls, chocolate chews that stuck to the roof of my mouth. Michael opened cans of beer—something I only knew about from the pages of James Joyce novels—and handed them out to the boys. I heard the faint voice of Teacher Agnes, chiding me. *Alcohol was created to weaken a woman's defenses,* she'd said. But I took a quick swig nonetheless.

———

"HE WON'T STOP LOOKING AT YOU," ARDEN SAID, LEANing against the wall. We'd settled into a corner to eat as much as we could. Scattered in front of us were cans of orange soda, thick, glossy pretzels, and jarred peaches. "I never believed anything Teacher Agnes said," she offered, tilting her head slightly. "But maybe the old bag was right. There is some kind of insanity in his eyes. It's like he wants to devour your soul or something."

I glanced up. Caleb was across the room, his eyes on me.

"Ew, Arden." I cringed. "Stop." But I was flooded with the memory of his lips against my forehead, my arms curled against his chest.

"You can *ew* all you want, but it's true. What did you do to him in that room—I only stepped out for a second!" She nudged me hard in the side and I laughed, nervously.

"Look what I found!" Charlie called out from the old dining room. He pulled at a dusty beige cloth, removing it like a magician, to expose an old piano. He put his fingers on its yellowing keys and tapped out a few tinny notes.

I leaned back, listening as the chords echoed in the first floor of the house. It reminded me of the summers at School, when Pip and I took piano lessons with Teacher Sheila. I would sit on the bench, pressing down the chords for "Amazing Grace" while Pip spun around behind me, pirouetting with each verse.

I turned back to Arden, about to explain how Pip sometimes mimed each word, hunching over for "wretch" or cupping her ear for "sound," but she was staring at the shelves in front of us, her mind somewhere else.

"What's wrong?"

"Eve, there's something I've been meaning to tell you . . ." She rubbed her forehead with her hand. "Those things I said at School—the stories about my parents taking me to the theater, of Thanksgiving dinners and their apartment in the City . . ." she whispered. "I made it up."

I sat up straighter. "What do you mean?"

She stared at her feet. Strands of black hair fell in her face. "In a way it was true—I *wasn't* like everyone at School," she said. Her lips were red and chapped. "I was an orphan before the plague even happened. I never had parents, not even in my life before."

Charlie banged out a few more notes on the piano and Arden looked up at me, waiting for my reaction.

"So the maids who laid out your clothes in the morning, the sterling locket your mother had promised you after you finished learning your trade, the house with the pond in the front and the bathtub with gold clawed feet?" I recalled the stories Arden had taunted us with. "Those were all lies?"

Arden nodded. I was confused, then angry. So many nights I'd laid on my bed and cried, wishing I'd had what Arden had. I wished it was *my* mother waiting for me in the City, like a gift yet to be opened.

"How could you do that?" I asked.

Arden turned to the window and stared at her reflection in the glass. "I don't know . . ."

"Everyone was so jealous of you, and you—"

"I know!" Arden cried. "But you all talked of your parents and families. I didn't even know what a family was. I had a grandfather, but he was nicer to his German shepherd than he was to me. It was a relief when he died."

I thought back to an eight-year-old Arden, telling everyone of the birthday parties her father threw her, how he'd built her a tree house, how they just had to get "situated" in the new City before she could join them. Arden had seemed so alive then, so animated.

"I'm sorry," she managed. "I'm so sorry."

Part of me wanted to get up, to get away, but the hurt in her eyes seemed real, the apology genuine. Yes, I had imagined reunions with my mother that would never happen. But I also had memories, keepsakes to turn over in my mind. How she had lifted me to hang candy canes on the Christmas tree. How we had painted with our fingers. Unlike Arden's stories, mine were real. "I'm sorry, too," I said, still unable to look at her.

We both sat there for some time, our shoulders touching as we watched the boys enjoy the raid. "I guess what I'm trying to say is . . . ," Arden said, finally breaking the silence, ". . . thank you." She stared straight ahead and pulled the thick green sweater around her neck.

"For what?" I asked, unable to keep the edge from my voice.

"For saving my life." Arden turned toward me. "I've never had anyone be so . . . *kind* to me." Tiny tremors rippled the skin of her chin, and then the tears spilled over her bottom lids.

I pressed my palm on her back to steady her. I wasn't used to seeing her upset. She was supposed to be the one who refused to cry. The one who killed rabbits. Who never once complained of her illness.

"It's okay." I patted the back of her head, working the black tangles from her short hair. "You don't have to thank me. You would have done the same for me."

Arden raised her head and nodded slowly, as if she weren't quite certain of that fact. "I didn't even know where I was sometimes. I just remember you combing my hair and washing my face and—" her voice cracked.

I pulled her into a hug. "It was nothing. Really." I felt her breath in my ear, choked with something wet. Her chest heaved beneath me, and I realized how hard she was crying. Her tears seeped through the wool of my sweater, slicking the skin of my shoulders. "It was nothing," I repeated.

"I know." Arden sniffed hard, not meeting my eyes. She pulled away, her hands wiping at her cheeks, blotting the skin around her hazel, bloodshot eyes. "I know."

During my life at School I always had Pip or Ruby by my side, calling me to supper or straightening my skirt when it was crooked. But for days in the wild, only the birds spoke to me. The stream was the only hand that touched me, the wind the only breath that blew the dust from my eyes. I learned the strange art of loneliness, the weathered yearning that swells and passes, swells and passes, when you walk a trail alone.

But Arden had long mastered it. In School, out of School. For too long.

I rested my hand on her shoulder, knowing then that I had misspoken—it wasn't nothing. To Arden, it was everything.

twenty

WE STAYED LIKE THAT, WITH ARDEN'S FOREHEAD ON my shoulder, until Caleb called out from the piano. "Come on you two," he said. "Stop being such . . . *girls*." He shot me a mischievous grin, his eyes shining.

Berkus, an older boy with shaggy gold hair, was playing "Heart and Soul," a remnant from his childhood. It was a simple tune with staccato notes, unlike the complicated chords we learned from Teacher Sheila, their sounds held by pressing the pedal. Michael and Aaron stood behind him, drumming their fingers along with the melody, bobbing their heads every so often. Even Leif's normally sullen stare was softer as he hunched over the piano, sipping contentedly on his beer.

I pulled Arden up. "You remember the Viennese waltz, don't you?" I asked.

During most classes, Arden had scribbled across the top of her notebook, making unrecognizable blobs in the margins of the page. But there was nowhere to hide when we danced. Every girl was partnered, every girl expected to keep her chin up, arms firm, as she glided across the lawn.

Arden's lips were still pressed into a line, but she let me pull her toward the piano. Berkus started the song again and I positioned my arms, gesturing for her to cradle her hand in mine. Caleb paused, his head cocked to the side, as he watched us. Then we stepped forward, the boys parting as I led her around the room, stepping lightly past the shelves, back straight, laughing.

"Heart and soul," I sang, "I saw you standing there, heart and soul, you look just like a bear."

"Those aren't the words!" Arden laughed. She let her head fall to the side, giving in to the turns. The boys cheered when I dipped Arden effortlessly to the floor and clapped when I spun us around in place. When I took her across the room, darting toward the kitchen, a serious expression seized her face. "About before—" She glanced over my shoulder at Kevin, who had ventured out onto the floor, beer in hand as he made a clumsy pirouette. "I think I'm still a little out of it, and that emotional stuff, it's probably just a side effect of—"

"I know," I interrupted. "Don't worry about it." There was a long pause, the piano notes ringing between us as we waltzed back toward the boys, our steps slower than before. Then she offered me a grateful smile.

When we spun our last spin, buoyed by the music and cheers, Caleb came toward us, gracefully stepping through the room. Behind him, Michael and Charlie were attempting wild moves, Michael spinning around the floor on his back.

"Can I have this dance?" Caleb asked. He extended his hand, palm up, waiting for mine.

"I don't know—*can* you?" I challenged, unable to resist myself. It was that silly grammatical slipup the Teachers always called us on in School.

Caleb took my hand in his own and gave it a firm tug, pulling me toward him. The boys hooted behind us. Aaron brought his fingers to his lips in a loud whistle.

"I guess I can." He smiled as my body pressed against his.

I rested my chin on his chest as Berkus gave up "Heart

and Soul" for a slower, more tentative song. The heel of Caleb's hand fit into the small of my back, resting on my spine. His breath warmed my neck. He wasn't a bad dancer, but it seemed strange to have someone lead me around the floor. I had always determined the steps, the direction—sent my partner off into quick, elegant spins.

"Are you glad you came?" he whispered in my ear.

The boys kept their eyes on us for a while, until they realized there would be nothing to see, only swaying back and forth, and the occasional step to the side. It was not the grand performance Arden and I had put on.

"I am," I said.

Berkus gave up his spot at the piano and climbed out onto the porch. A few others followed, along with Arden, and they all headed to the makeshift pool outside.

"I'm glad you came, too." Caleb adjusted his body, moving closer so I fit in the grooves of his form. My eyelids lowered, the storehouse disappearing from view. I felt only the warmth of his chest next to mine. It would be so easy to stay here, like this, to spend the days in the dugout and the nights on raids with Caleb. The visions kept coming to me whenever my mind quieted, the images piled one on top of another. Arden and I would take care of Benny and Silas, making sure their hands were clean, teaching them to read and write. We'd work with them until they were scrawling full paragraphs across the mud walls and explaining the themes of *A Winter's Tale*. With their new skills, the older boys could start organizing, sending out messages to other escaped orphans, and making further plans with Moss.

As for Caleb and me . . . all I wanted was more of this. The closeness of my chin on his shoulder, his hand resting on my back, the ease of being together, our bodies speaking even in silence.

"I've been thinking . . ." I said, pulling my head back to look at him.

Outside, Michael sprang off the rotting deck and into the air. "Bombs away!" he cried, leaving only a giant splash in his wake. He wiped some green muck from his face as he reached a rusty ladder. "Come on in, the sludge is warm!"

Caleb laughed and then turned back to me. "You've been thinking . . . ?"

"Califia," I said, my voice thin with sudden nerves. "It seems pointless to go all the way there, now, risking our lives, when Arden and I could just live in the dugout. We're safe here. She could help me teach the boys, and . . ." I looked into his green eyes hopefully. "And we'd be together—"

Caleb's face tensed. He took a step back, breaking us apart. "Eve . . ."

I could feel every inch between us now, the space growing. Had he misunderstood? I cleared my throat. "I want to stay. I want to live at the camp, with you."

He rubbed the back of his neck and sighed. "I don't think that's a good idea." He lowered his voice as he spoke, his eyes darting outside to where the boys stood on the rotted porch, daring each other to jump.

"The King's men are still after you. If they find us . . . the boys would be punished. And you'll never be completely safe . . ."

I stepped away, widening the space between us even farther. Each word hit me in the chest, banging on the door to my heart, which had curled up inside itself and gone to sleep.

He didn't want me here.

Of course he didn't. It didn't matter how he said it, what words he used to explain it away. I closed my eyes and saw Teachers Agnes, her hands shaking. *He didn't want me.* She looked out the window, the water running down the deep creases in her face as if he had just left her a moment ago. *I was such a fool. He never wanted me.*

Caleb reached for my arm but I shook him off. "Don't touch me," I said, backing away.

He was a man, he was always a man, with all his faults and tiny deceptions. And I had let him hold me, let my lips kiss his, given in to all the temptations. I had been a fool.

"I understand exactly what's going on here. This was a game to you, wasn't it?"

He shook his head, face pallid. "No, you're not listening to me. I want you to stay, but you can't—it's not safe." He reached for me again but I dodged his hand. *You want to believe the lies,* Teacher Agnes had said. *It is the believer's fault for believing.*

"Please—just leave me alone!" I cried as he reached for me again. My voice echoed in the empty storehouse. Charlie turned, his hand on the window frame. The remaining boys on the porch looked up.

Caleb rubbed at the space between his brows. "We'll talk about this later, when we're back in the dugout. I care about you, but—"

"You care about yourself," I snapped.

His head jerked back, as if I'd slapped him in the face. Slowly he turned, climbed out onto the porch, and disappeared among the shadows of the others. The boys quietly whispered and then surveyed the pool again, leaping into the dark water.

The room around me expanded, the air cooler without him there. I sat down at the piano, tapping out a long, scratchy C. I closed my eyes as each note of Beethoven's "Moonlight Sonata" rang out in the storehouse, strained and out of tune. As I approached the second theme, tears escaped from my eyes. I paused, wiping them away.

"What was that about?" a voice asked behind me. Leif came down the stairs, the wood creaking with each step. Before I could respond, he collapsed onto the warped bench beside me.

"Nothing," I said quickly. I turned my gaze to the upper floors. "What were you doing up there?"

Leif dug his fingernails into his beer can until the metal gave way. "Just looking around." He tilted his head and curled his lips.

I'd grown accustomed to his presence around camp, to squeezing past him in the narrow corridors or acknowledging him with a nod. But right now, the last thing I wanted was another man to talk to. I kept playing the notes, trying to ignore him, but he pulled a paper from his pocket and set it in front of me as though it were sheet music.

My fingers froze on the keys.

"Where did you get that?" I asked. I grabbed the paper.

UPDATE: EVE WAS LAST SEEN HEADING NORTH-
WEST, TOWARD LAKE TAHOE AREA. TRAVELING ON
HORSEBACK WITH ANOTHER FEMALE AND A MALE,
BETWEEN SEVENTEEN AND TWENTY YEARS OLD. IF
SPOTTED, CONTACT THE NORTHWEST OUTPOST. SHE
IS TO BE DELIVERED DIRECTLY TO THE KING.

"I can explain. I'm—"

"Don't bother." Leif rested his arm on the piano ledge and pulled in another sip of his beer. His black eyes met mine. "Technically I'm a fugitive, too. I'm sure the King would want me back in his camp, lugging cement blocks on my back like a donkey."

I crumpled the paper in my hand. I didn't know whether to thank Leif, or to apologize. I'd moved into his camp, a stranger, put them all in danger, and lied about it. "We're just stopping through, on our way to Califia."

Leif appraised me, but this time there was no judgment in his gaze, simply interest. "I never thought you, of all people, would be hunted by the King. What is it you did? Killed a guard? Held a Teacher hostage? He wouldn't want you for just running away." He was smiling now, his expression playful. I couldn't imagine being proud of killing someone, but he seemed charmed, my image suddenly textured in his view, these new shades creating an unexpected depth.

"I'd rather not say." I felt queasy as I thought of the City, and the man whose face looked out from that gilded frame at School.

He pressed down on the keys, hard, the notes sounding out in the still air. I shook my head. "I know about the terrible things they do, maybe more than anyone. It's torture living like weasels underground, knowing about the feasts in the City of Sand, the resorts and swimming pools filled with purified water. And you couldn't imagine the camps." He stopped playing, his gaze fixed on a clock above the piano. Moisture was trapped inside its face, and its hands were stopped at 11:11. "I had a brother, Asher—"

"I know," I said softly. The outside sounds flooded in. The boys were running around in the woods, their voices livened by a game of tag. "Caleb mentioned . . ." I looked out the window but he wasn't there, only darkness.

Leif ran his fingers along the piano, tracing the grain of the wood. "*Asher*. It's been so long since I spoke his name," he said, almost to himself. "Our mother used to play the piano for us. I remember being under the dining room table with him, watching our father's feet hanging over the couch as he read his books, and my mother pressing on those pedals. We'd take our plastic tanks and trucks and we'd battle with each other as she played." He pinched the tab of the can, moving it back and forth.

"Do you ever think of that, what it was like before the plague?" he said.

I could barely swallow. I remembered the way my mother and I held hands, wrapping my palm around her pinky finger as she took me through the aisles of the supermarket. How she kissed the soles of my feet, or how I sat in her closet while she changed, hiding among the dresses and pants, which held the lovely smell of her.

"Yes," I said. "Sometimes." *All the time*, I thought. *All the time.*

Leif pressed his lips together, as if considering what I'd said. His fingers wandered around on the keys, playing the occasional note. "Da dum dum dum," he sang slowly, tentatively. A few more notes escaped, creating a familiar string of melody. "Do you know that song?" he asked, turning toward me.

"Pachelbel's Canon," I said as I pressed down on the

first notes. It was still recognizable, even out of tune. "I learned it in School."

"That's the song she always played." He smiled at the wall but it was clear he was looking through it, at a different scene altogether.

I kept playing, leaning forward, letting the song evolve from one melody to the next. I felt the accumulation of the past hours, now a thick melancholy that polluted everything. Watching Caleb come up the shore, the quiet of the room as our lips touched, his heartbeat through his shirt, that dance. Everything was different now, colored in a different light. I wouldn't be with him. In the dugout or elsewhere. Arden and I would leave soon, maybe tomorrow. It would all come to an end.

What did I get out of it? Teacher Agnes had asked, to no one in particular. *What was the point of it all?*

twenty-one

THE STOREHOUSE WAS QUIET. LIGHT CAME IN THROUGH the windows, casting shadows on the shelves, stacked with old blankets and medical supplies. The containers of fuel filled the room with the sickening stink of gasoline. We had camped out for the night, the boys collapsing in heaps on the downstairs floor. Arden slept in the room next door.

I shifted, turned over, pounded at my makeshift bed of quilts and lumpy pillows, unable to stop thinking about Caleb. Our conversation, his retreat to the porch. After leaving Leif on the piano bench, his hand squeezing mine in thanks, I'd found Arden outside near the pool. As the boys slowed, overcome by the haze of the beer and sugar, Caleb watched me from a distance, never saying anything. When Arden pulled me upstairs, layering the wood planks with pillows and urging me to rest, I couldn't. Even now.

Hours had passed. Outside, the only sound was the wind in the trees, the occasional snap of a branch. I wondered if I had been wrong. The reaction a reflex, like those physicals at School, my leg jerking out when I felt the doctor's hammer on my knee. He had said something about my safety. He had said something about him caring. Then I had yelled, pushed him away. What would have happened if he had continued? I was replaying it, imagining his face, when the door opened and a figure appeared behind the wood shelves.

"Eve?"

"Caleb?" I asked, sitting up.

He stumbled and several boxes hit the ground. He crept forward, turning past the corner, kneeling onto the edge of my bed. Then he reached for my hand.

"About before . . ." I started. The silence swelled between us.

His hand squeezed my hand. Then, in a moment, he was right there, his lips against mine. I leaned in but there was no soft give, only urgency. He pushed forward, forcing my head back. I opened my eyes. I could barely make out his face in the moonlight, squeezed in concentration. His palms were rough against my skin. Everything felt strange, terrible—*wrong.*

I reached up, trying to ease him off when I felt the thick bun nestled at the nape of his neck. "No!" I yelled, pulling my face away. "No!" But Leif pushed forward, settling his body on the floor beside me, the wood groaning under his weight.

His mouth covered my lips. I could taste the bitter rot of alcohol on his tongue. He ran his hands over my shoulders and down my arms. I tried to scream again, but his mouth was over mine. No sound escaped.

I struggled. My fists landed against Leif's chest, but he pulled me closer. He kept kissing me, the thick slime of his mouth coating my chin. I jerked away, rolling my shoulders to the side, trying to escape. But everywhere I went he found me, his breath hot and musty on my skin.

So many things had been stolen from me: my mother, the house with the blue shingles where I had taken my first steps, those finished canvases stacked against the classroom wall. But this was the most painful of all, the control ripped from my grasp. *No,* he seemed to say, with each urgent grope. *Even your body is not yours.*

Tears escaped my eyes, forming shallow pools in my ears. He kissed my neck, his hands roaming the length of my body. I was drowning. Fear surrounded me, growing so that I was left with no choice: I had to take it in. My chest bucked, my feet seized. I was choking on my own panic.

Somewhere, far above the surface, I heard the murmurs of voices. "What's going on?" someone asked. "She was yelling." The bright light of a flashlight beam settled first on my legs, then on my wet face, and finally on Leif, his eyes in a half-closed daze.

"You monster," Caleb growled. He picked Leif up by his underarms and heaved him into the side of one of the shelves. Metal boxes clattered and fell, sending hundreds of matches skittering across the floor.

Aaron and Michael appeared in the doorway, their flashlights illuminating the darkness. Leif struggled to his feet. He plowed forward, landing his shoulder into Caleb's rib cage. Caleb winced in pain as he slammed against the wall.

"Enough, Leif!" he cried, but Leif threw another punch, landing hard in Caleb's jaw. I folded myself into the far corner of the room, trapped.

Leif staggered to the side, his movements loose from

all the alcohol. "Come on, you've always wanted to lead," he slurred. Strands of black hair hung in his face and I wondered if he'd gone to sleep at all, or if this whole time he'd been downstairs, working through the last of the tin cans. "So be the leader, Caleb. See how you like it."

Leif gestured wildly at the doorway. The commotion had awoken the rest of the boys and they huddled together, straining to watch. Kevin pulled on his cracked glasses, as if unsure of what he'd seen.

Leif circled Caleb, his arms out at his sides. The person who had sat next to me on the bench, swaying with the music, was no longer here. Something had taken hold of him, something terrifying and primal. "Come on," he urged again, lunging in Caleb's face. "Now's your chance to be a man."

Caleb sprung forward. In one swift motion he grabbed Leif's arm, twisted, and pushed him to the floor. Leif fell hard, his cheek meeting the wood with a horrible *whack*. A pool of blood spread out underneath his face and I could see, even in the dark, that his lip had busted open.

"She wanted to be with me." He spit blood as he spoke, covering the floor in spatter. "Why do you think she was sitting with me before? Why do you think she was talking to me? She wanted me. Not you—*me*." The certainty in his voice was tinged with anger. I slunk back against the wall, afraid even now, with his body limp on the floor.

Caleb turned toward me, his face wrought with confusion. "Is that true?"

My hands trembled violently and tears streamed down my face. What Leif had done was wrong. And yet . . . I had sat beside him on the piano, playing for him. I had allowed his shoulder to press close as he spoke of his family. I had let his hand squeeze mine. Had I given him some unspoken invitation? Had my kindness seemed like something more?

"I don't know," I said, covering my mouth with my hand.

"You don't know?" Caleb asked. His grasp tightened around Leif's arm, pushing him farther into the ground. He glared at me from under his brows, the lightness I had loved about his face disappearing. I wanted him to stop, to look away, to give me just one moment to think.

But he just stared, waiting for an answer. I started to sob, my chest rocking as I lost myself in each waterlogged breath.

"Eve! What happened? Are you okay?" Arden pushed through the crowd of boys and ran to my side. She held me up, gasping at the slight rip in my sweater. "I heard the noise and—" she paused, noticing Caleb's face. He shook his head from side to side, a nearly imperceptible move-ment, but a constant, unmistakable no.

He stood, leaving Leif on the floor, the black puddle of blood beneath him. Then he pushed through Michael and Aaron and down the stairs, not looking back.

"Caleb!" I yelled, sobered by his sudden absence. The crowd parted and I followed him out the door, but when I reached the bottom of the stairs there was only stale air and the crunch of garbage beneath my feet. The rest of the storehouse was dark as I felt around, looking for the entrance. "Caleb!" I called again.

Finally I spotted the glowing woods, just visible through the front door. There, out in the clearing, Caleb was climbing onto his horse, a black figure under a star-spotted sky.

"Don't leave! Please!" I yelled, stepping outside. But he was already pulling at the reins, turning the horse away.

I stood watching, my feet rooted in the dirt. I didn't notice when Arden joined my side. I didn't hear Kevin and Michael's voices, calling from the upstairs window, beckoning him back.

I knew only sadness as he rode through the woods, shrinking on the horizon, until the night swallowed him whole.

twenty-two

"WE SHOULD LEAVE," ARDEN WHISPERED. SHE WAS SIT-ting in our cavernous mudroom. "Get back on the road to Califia. It's not safe here anymore."

We'd left the storehouse before dawn, the horses loaded with sacks of candy, fuel, blankets, and condensed milk. All the while Leif was a menacing presence, his face bandaged from the night before. I shook from the thought of his lips smashing against mine, the sour stink of beer on his breath. I kept seeing his face in the glow of the flashlight, his eyes squeezed shut, his body a falling boulder, crushing me under its weight.

When we returned to the dugout, Caleb's room had

not been touched. The weathered books were stacked in piles. The bed was covered with the thin red blanket and the armchair was still in the corner, the cushion dipping where he once sat.

"We can't just go," I said, pressing my back into the cold mud wall. Part of me was tied to the idea of living here, the knot of it not yet loose. "At least not until Caleb comes back."

Arden's fingers wandered through her hair, yanking at the tangled black ends. "I don't like the way Leif has been looking at us." There were puffy crescents under her eyes from the night before. She'd stayed awake, barring the door with an overturned shelf, keeping watch until I finally fell asleep.

"I can't leave like this." My thoughts kept returning to the middle of the storehouse, where I'd thrown Caleb's arm from mine. We hadn't really discussed anything; I'd been too upset to think straight. Then Leif was beside me, his fingers drumming on the wood of the piano, misinterpreting my kindness as an invitation. I wished that I hadn't uttered those three fatal words—*I don't know.*

I *did* know, but it was impossible to explain all the dark emotions I'd encountered the night before. They came at me so fast there was no time to pick each one up, to hold it and know it for what it was.

But now, sitting in the cavern with Arden, I grew even more certain of one thing: "I didn't want to be with Leif."

Arden's face softened. She pulled me into a tight embrace, her arms squeezing any guilt from my body. "Of course you didn't. That was never a question."

I spoke into her shoulder, the musty smell of her sweater enveloping me. "I just hate that Caleb thinks I would ever—"

"I know," Arden said, rubbing my back.

I pressed the water from my eyes. When I was in my sixth year, I was furious at Ruby for telling Pip I'd been "bragging" about my grades. Instead of saying how I'd felt, I didn't speak to her for two weeks. I let the wound fester and grow, feeding on the silence between us. I learned then a crucial truth: that a relationship between two people can be judged by the list of things unspoken between them. I longed to see Caleb now, if only to tell him all that I was feeling. That I'd been wounded by his words. That I was thankful for what he did, that I'd been frightened and confused. That it wasn't Leif who I wanted.

Despite myself, despite all those hours being tested on the

Dangers of Boys and Men, I had feelings for him. Only him.

My head was still resting on Arden's shoulder when the room began to shake, tiny tremors working their way inside my rib cage. "What is it?"

"Earthquake!" Silas yelled as he sprinted past our room, clutching Benny's hand. He nearly tripped on his oversized shorts, their hem around his ankles, the waist cinched with rope. "Get out! Get out!"

A few of the younger boys started down the twisting corridor, filing through as though they'd practiced the drill several times before.

"An earthquake?" I asked, placing a palm on the shaking wall. "It can't be." We'd experienced them at School, the jolting that sometimes woke us in the middle of the night. This vibrating was subtle and nowhere near as strong.

"Let's not wait to find out," Arden said, pulling me to the door.

We followed the younger boys as they wormed their way through the dugout, finally spilling out onto the rocky clearing in the side of the hill. There, atop a large mound of dirt, was a giant black truck, its wheels nearly four feet high. I could barely hear over the roar of the engine.

"Cool!" Silas mouthed. In the bright morning light he was so much paler than everyone else, his skin unaccustomed to the sun. He plugged his ears with his fingers.

Benny smiled up at me, revealing the gap in his teeth. "It's a big truck!" he shouted.

But I felt only growing fear as I eyed the shadowy figure in the front seat. This massive vehicle, with its dirt-spattered sides and the caved-in front bumper, looked nothing like the Jeeps from School. The only automobiles I'd ever seen belonged to the government. The King rationed oil, and most people didn't have the patience to go from abandoned car to abandoned car, trying to siphon gas.

Some of the older boys had returned from hunting to see the commotion, their horses appearing at the edge of the clearing. Leif was among them, his movements unhurried. I was thankful when Michael, Aaron, and Kevin dismounted and surrounded the truck, their spears pointing at the cab.

Finally, the engine shut off, leaving behind a dull humming in my ears. "Weapons down!" Leif called. One by one the boys pulled back.

The side door flew open and a giant steel-tipped boot stepped out onto the gravel hillside. I shrunk back at the sight of the man. He was over six feet tall, with oiled hair that fell past his shoulders. He wore a beaten black leather jacket. Sweat ran from his forehead to the handkerchief at his neck. His gaze met mine and he smiled, a smile that caused my entire body to seize in fear. His teeth were cracked yellow stumps.

Silas threw his tiny arms around my legs. "Who is he?" he asked.

But the man was already stalking toward me, puckering his dirt-caked lips. The older boys stood at the edge of the clearing, watching him cross, uncertain what to do. He didn't stop until he was right in front of me, engulfing me in his massive shadow.

"Hello, my little lady," he hissed in my ear.

I backed away but he grabbed my arm, yanking me forward. His clothes were soaked with mud and old sweat. The stench made my stomach lurch.

Michael and Kevin ran to my side. Kevin angled his spear at the stranger's throat. "Get off her!" he yelled.

But the man grabbed the wood stick, his fist clenched tight as he turned toward Leif. "This is the one?"

Leif's face was calm. "She's wanted by the King," he announced, glancing around at the boys. My spine straightened at the words. The truth was being turned against me, Leif's humiliation from last night transformed into something sinister. "She's a fugitive, and she's put us all in danger long enough. Fletcher is taking her to the troops."

"He is not!" Arden yelled, landing her hands into the man's stocky side. I turned to run, but his grip was firm, crushing my wrist. He reached for Arden and caught her thin arm, both of us struggling to free ourselves from his grasp.

"Two for the price of one," Fletcher laughed, flecks of spit flying as he pulled us toward the truck.

"No! She can't go!" Benny cried. "Please, Leif!"

"You can't let him do this," Michael said, turning to Leif. He kept his hand on his spear.

"Stop!" a few of the new Hunters yelled, while Silas ran after me, his hands pulling at my baggy gray sweater. In the panic I saw only flashes: Benny's crumpled face, Kevin pushing forward, Aaron falling in the dirt, his side scraped red. Arden bit down on Fletcher's hand and I suddenly realized what was in the back of his truck: a cage, with a frail girl screaming out between the bars.

Leif spotted her at the same time. His expression shifted as he took in Fletcher's hand on Arden's wrist. "Wait," he muttered. He ran toward the truck and banged on its metal side in frustration. "Who is this? What's going on?"

Fletcher didn't flinch. He dragged us by the wrists, our feet scraping against the rocks. "That's not your concern. You wanted her gone and she's going." he huffed.

My stomach rocked, the breakfast of quail eggs rising in the back of my throat. I choked it down, pulling and twisting my arm, trying to break free. Whatever sick agreement Leif had made, this had spiraled beyond his control.

"Where are the medicines? Where is the payment?" Leif charged forward, his face crimson. Michael and Aaron followed his lead, taking tentative steps with their spears in hand. I closed my eyes, waiting for them to strike, but the giant brute pulled a gun from his belt and fired it at the sky. The boys fell back, surprised by the loud *pop!*

"Now listen good," Fletcher growled. He cleared his throat, hocking a giant greenish blob into the dirt. "I'm taking my prize here and leaving, and if I have to shoot someone dead to do it, I goddamn will. You hear me?"

Silas held his hand in his mouth and let out a slow, painful moan. He kept his eyes on me as I was dragged, my heels bloody against the ground, toward the truck.

Arden screamed, hurling her fists against the bounty

hunter's arm. "You are an animal!" she yelled. "Let me go!"

Arden kept on, trying to squirm free, refusing to believe what was happening, but I knew it was over. Our fists were no match for a gun. The boys stared down at their weapons, as if betrayed. The carved bones seemed so futile now.

I kept my gaze on Silas and Benny, their tiny bodies heaving with sobs. Benny tugged on Leif's hand, yanking down hard, but Leif just stared ahead, his bewildered black eyes moving slowly around the landscape.

"It's okay!" I cried out to Benny and Silas, trying to smile despite the panic. "I'm going to be okay. Don't worry about me." I hoped they would believe me.

Fletcher opened the padlock on the truck and lowered the gun at us, gesturing for us both to get inside. I climbed up, his free hand rough on my skin. The bed of the truck was hot from the midday sun. The girl was slumped in the corner, her sticklike arms folded across each other. She bolted upright when the crate opened, renewed with terror.

"Help! Help me!" she screamed, her hands stretching out between the bars, to where Michael and Aaron stood.

They looked at her and back to the gun. When they stepped forward, Leif rested his arm across their chests, holding them in place.

"You did this, Leif!" Arden screamed, pressing her face through the bars and leveling a finger at him. "This is your fault."

Fletcher slammed into the truck.

"We need the payment!" Leif spat, as he approached. "That was the deal! I trusted you!" He ran to the cab, his fists pounding on its dented door.

Fletcher looked over the window, the glass shattered in a circle from where a bullet had ripped through. "This is the wild." He gestured with his gun as he spoke. "Don't trust anyone, boy." He smiled, his cracked lips bleeding, and started the engine.

I held the thin bars, pushing against them, wishing they would give under my weight. The sun was too hot on my skin, the cage too small, the thin blanket in the corner caked with vomit. Arden's screams rocked me, doubling my sadness. Leif had betrayed us. Caleb was gone. Whatever time I had spent in the night, wondering if I should stay, for how long—it had all been pointless. What did I want? What did Caleb want? It didn't matter.

We were going now. The decision made for me. I kicked against the crate's door and scraped my fingernails against the lock. I shrieked and cried and begged, but nothing—not one thing—could change that simple fact.

The truck started down the rocky cliff, sending us sliding around inside. The older boys pushed back, trying to corral Benny and Silas toward camp as the giant machine pitched and heaved over the landscape, wheeling around toward the lake. I kept my eyes on the boys, on Aaron, who was clutching Leif's arm, begging him to do something, and Kevin, who launched his spear in the air, its arc falling three yards short of the truck's cab. I kept my eyes on the dugout, its dark mouth closing behind the short brush.

Leif gripped Benny's shoulders to hold him back, but he broke free and chased the truck, pumping his tiny arms and legs with great fury.

"I love you!" he called out, when he was just ten feet away. I gripped the metal bars, my throat choked with emotion.

"I love you!" Silas cried, as he followed.

They both kept after us, sprinting wildly behind the cage. I watched their mouths moving, saying those words over and again, as the truck bounded through the woods and their small bodies disappeared, unreachable, behind the trees.

twenty-three

THE TRUCK CLIMBED THE TANGLED LANDSCAPE, RUSH-
ing through fields of weeds and overgrown brush, until
we came to a broken road. Its wheels spun faster, and dust
bloomed thicker around its fenders. The sun heated the
metal cage, making its bars painful to touch.

After an hour I didn't recognize the forest that spread
out beyond the rocky path. Even the sky seemed foreign,
its great blue expanse birdless and lonely.

"I knew it," Arden said finally. Her pale skin was covered with a thin layer of dirt. "Leif was just waiting to
sell us out, for what?" She shielded her eyes from the sun.
"Some medical supplies and a cut of ransom money?"

"He wanted me gone," I said. "I doubt the supplies mattered."

I wondered how it had happened, if he'd searched the black storehouse looking for a radio. Or perhaps he had stumbled upon it looking for a bandage, trying to stop the blood from his mouth.

I wondered, too, when Caleb would realize I'd been taken. Would he dismount his horse by the edge of the woods, seeing Benny and Silas sobbing near the dugout entrance? Would he kneel down, inspecting the long tracks in the dirt where my heels had been dragged, his face turning toward Leif? Would he miss me? Would he care?

None of it mattered. It was over. No way to escape the bars, the burning sun, this man with the cracked yellow teeth. I was trapped again, new walls holding me in, bringing me to the King. the City gates would open and close behind me, another cage.

Cage after cage after cage.

Beyond the bars the world moved past, faster than I'd ever seen it before. Trees. Yellow flowers that lined the road. Old houses, their roofs caved in. I glimpsed deer and rabbits, bent bicycles, rusted cars, and wild dogs. They all slipped away, too fast, like water down a drain. *I am going to the City of Sand,* I kept thinking, as though the repetition could numb me. *I am being taken to the King. I will never see Caleb again.*

Arden watched the landscape, her eyes watery. She had tried so hard to free herself of School. She'd come this far—all for what? To be caught in this net because of me? No doubt she was thinking of that dumb choice she'd made weeks ago in that cottage, regretting she ever agreed to let me stay on with her.

"I'm sorry," I said, my voice choked. "I'm so sorry, Arden. You must wish you hadn't ever let me come with you."

"No." Arden wrapped her fingers around the bars. Her pale skin was pink from just an hour in the sun. "Not at all, Eve." She turned to me and her hazel eyes glistened with tears.

Just then, the girl in the corner shifted, sat up, and rubbed her face. She'd been too hysterical to talk to us after we left the dugout. Instead she'd curled up on the hot metal bed and fallen asleep, her eyelids twitching with nightmares.

"Who are you?" she asked, wincing as her skin touched the bars.

"I'm Eve. This is Arden," I said, pointing across the

cage. In the cab of the truck, Fletcher turned up the music, howling along to a dreadful, skipping song. *I love rock 'n' roll-oll-oll-oll*, it went, *put another dime in-in the jukebox, baby.*

The girl reached out her thin hand for us to shake. "I'm Lark."

"What School are you from?" I asked, noticing her jumper. It was cut in the same square shape of ours, but it was blue instead of gray.

"It was West, I think." She rubbed her hands through her thick black hair. She looked about thirteen, with arms so thin her shoulder bones jutted out in two defined knots. Her deep brown skin cracked and peeled around her elbows and knees. "38°35'N, 121°30'W, is what the Teachers called it."

I knew those numbers meant something. Our Teachers used them when they referred to School, but I had never figured out exactly what. We'd always been 39°30'N, 119°49'W.

"So you escaped," Arden said.

"I needed to get out of there." The girl pressed back into the corner of the cage, not meeting our eyes.

I glanced across to Arden, relieved that we weren't the only girls who knew the truth about the Schools. I studied

Lark's legs, which were scraped red in places, the same way mine had been those first days in the wild. Mosquito bites dotted her arms and there was a hole in one of her canvas shoes, exposing her big toe.

"How did you get here?" I asked.

Lark rubbed at the skin around her eyes, where her tears had dried, leaving only fine patches of white salt. "I found a break in one of the metal fences. It was barely a foot wide and they were about to repair it. They'd boarded it up for the night to keep the dogs away, but I snuck through." She pointed to the side of her jumper, where the fabric was torn, exposing her bare hip. "Then I ran until I found a house to sleep in. I think that was four days ago, but I'm not sure."

"Where'd he find you?" Arden asked, nodding to Fletcher. He hung his meaty arm out the window, throwing it up in time with the words. *So come and take your time and dance with-with me!*

Lark wrapped her arms around her legs, curling herself into a tight ball. "I saw this jug of water sitting out on the road. I was so thirsty, I had been walking the whole day in the sun. It was a trap though. He must've been following me."

The truck hit a bump, sending my stomach toward my

heart. I clung to the bars, even though they stung the soft flesh of my palms. "Did you tell anyone else about the breeding?" I asked. "Are there others trying to escape?"

Lark looked up, confusion knitting her brow. "Breeding? What are you talking about?"

"The sows," Arden said loudly, making sure the word was audible even over the music and the engine. Still, there was no recognition in Lark's face. "That's why you left—you were going to be used for breeding."

Lark dug her heels into the metal truck bed, pushing her back straight. "No—" she said, an edge in her voice. "I left because of this." She turned, showing us the blueish-black lines that marked the skin on the back of her bicep. It was the unmistakable imprint of fingers. "She waited for the others to leave before she hit me. I was going to find a different School—someplace better. I never want to see that woman again."

Arden opened her mouth to speak, eager to tell Lark of the vitamins and fertility treatments and the horrible rooms with metal beds, but I held up my hand. Of all the things I could rely on Arden for, sensitivity was not one of them.

"Lark," I said slowly, meeting the young girl's gaze. "The girls in those Schools—I was one of them—were never going to learn a trade. Out here we're called sows, and we were meant to birth children. As many as we could, to populate the City of Sand."

Arden couldn't help herself any longer. "They are taking us to the City, and Eve is going to be given to the King and then you and I are going right back to those Schools, right back to those beds." Her voice cracked as she said it.

"No," Lark said. She bit down hard on her fingertip and spit the cracked skin aside. "That's not possible."

"I didn't want to believe it either, but I saw them—"

"You saw wrong," Lark snapped. She sat forward on her knees. "You don't know what you're talking about. Headmistress is evil . . . but that isn't possible." She shook her head. "Maybe it was just your School. They wouldn't do that to us—for what?"

Arden lunged forward, her hand closing around Lark's thin arm. "Listen to us," she hissed. Lark flinched at her hot breath. "Listen to what we're saying. They need to populate the City. How do you think they're going to do that? How?"

"Get off me," Lark said, shaking her arm. "You're crazy." But as she slunk into the corner, her voice was softer, less certain.

"If you want to be some sow for the rest of your life, then you can," Arden went on. She leveled a finger at Lark. "But we're not going back to the Schools, I won't, I'm not going to—" Her mouth twisted before she could get the words out. When she sat down her body seemed so much smaller and weaker than before.

I felt someone watching us and I turned, meeting Fletcher's gaze in the dusty rearview mirror. The music faded and he slid open the back window of the cab.

"Don't you worry, my pretty sweetheart," he said. "I'm not taking you back to School." He lowered the mirror to look at Arden's bare legs. "Three ladies . . . so pure? I could get *much* more for you elsewhere."

With that he dialed up the music again, rapping his fingers against the side door. *Come an' take-ake-ake your time-ime and dance with me! Ow!*

Arden didn't speak. Instead she tried the metal lock on the cage again, banging at it until her fingers were red. The landscape whipped by us, a blur of yellow dirt. The tree branches reached toward the road like gnarled fingers.

"What does he mean?" Lark asked, looking up at me. Her lower lip trembled as she spoke.

I hated her right then, this stranger, for being so

familiar to me. In her face I saw someone I used to be, a girl who was so sure of the purpose of School, with its walls and its rules and the orderly lines that filed past the bedrooms and into the dining hall. She thought she could go somewhere else and be given something different, something better. Another future.

"You're getting your wish," I said, unable to stop the cold words from escaping my lips. "You're not going to see the Headmistress again."

twenty-four

WE SAT IN THAT TRUCK FOR HOURS, OUR LUNGS CAKED
with dirt. Even the sun abandoned us, sinking low
between the trees. We'd fallen in and out of sleep, thinking we had time—time to prepare, time to escape—but
then the gadget at Fletcher's belt called out, waking us.

"Fletcher, you devil! What's your ETA? I have too
much demand and not enough supply."

I was pressed into one corner. Lark slept in the other,
and Arden curled up in a ball at my side, their faces just
visible in the reddish glow from the taillights.

Fletcher brought the strange radio to his mouth, pushing a button on its side to stop the static. "Cool your

crotch," he chuckled. "I'm camping for the night. We'll be there in the morning."

Static filled the air, then a callous laugh. "Tell me what you got. Come on, give the boys a little preview."

I imagined the same men I'd seen by the shack, their hides tanned to a leathery brown, gathered under a tarp in camp, awaiting our arrival. I pressed my nose through the bars, desperate for more air.

"They're all steamers," Fletcher offered, his eyes glancing at us in the rearview mirror. "I'll give them to you tomorrow, you crud guzzler." He threw the radio down and turned his music on again.

Back at School, I had once argued for the goodness of people, and the great capacity for change. But listening to him laugh, the radio held lightly in his hand, I sensed only depravity. One thing Teacher Agnes had said *was* true, even now: Some men saw women purely as a commodity. Like fuel, rice, or canned meat.

Arden watched me from the side of the cage, turned so her back was to him. "We have to get out of here," she whispered. "Tonight."

"But he'll kill us," Lark said, pulling the worn blanket over her legs.

"We're already dead," Arden snapped.

I nodded, knowing that she was right. I had felt it in the storehouse with Leif, my spirit bending, bending, agonizingly close to a break. Fletcher would not change his mind. He would not show some sudden decency. There would be no moral awakening in the middle of the night.

I shifted toward Lark and Arden, covering the side of my face with my hair so Fletcher would not see my lips move if he glanced toward us.

"We can go when he sets up camp," I said, my nerves awakening.

I looked out beyond the bars, hoping to see a road sign, an arrow, some indicator of where we were, but there was only darkness.

—⊹—

HOURS LATER, THE TRUCK PULLED OFF THE ROAD, ITS tires bumping over rocks and broken tree limbs. We stopped in a clearing. The sky was overcast, with no moon in sight. The landscape had changed. The thick trees gave way to open land, short shrubs, and sand that glowed red in the headlights. Rock formations towered above us, something between mountains and cliffs, their shapes cutting strange shadows in the stars. Fletcher climbed out, stretched his arms, then turned to urinate in the short brush.

"Just do what we said," Arden whispered, grabbing Lark's wrist.

"I know," she said, pulling away. Her voice was rigid. "You told me already."

"We need to go to the bathroom." I banged against the metal bars. "Please, we need to get out now."

Fletcher zipped up his pants. "What?"

"She said," Arden continued, wiping her black hair off her forehead, "we need to take a piss."

Fletcher nodded, as though he understood that wording much better. He shined a flashlight into the cage, then out into the shrubs, where a battered house stood at the base of the giant rocks. "All of yous?"

"All of us," Arden responded. Even Lark offered a convincing nod.

Fletcher moved the beam over Arden's face, then Lark's, then mine. I squinted at the stinging light. "You've got two minutes. You can go over there, in the woods." His flashlight moved over the patch of charred trees, black and twisted from where a fire had swept through. "But if you dare even take one step without my permission—" He pulled his gun from his belt, wielding it in the air.

Lark's breaths quickened as Fletcher opened the giant padlock. We filed out, Arden first, then me, then Lark.

Fletcher kept the beam on our backs as we made our way to the trees.

The woods looked more menacing in the glow of the flashlight. The branches, now stripped of their bark and leaves, reached toward us, beckoning us inside.

"Not yet," I whispered, unsure if it was Lark or myself who needed reminding. We took slow, careful steps through the short brush. New growth shot up between the ashy roots, tall grass and ferns, hopeful signs of resilience.

As we reached the edge of the tree line, Arden turned to me. Her gaze softened. Her mouth curled slightly, a sort-of smile perceptible only to me. *This may be goodbye*, she seemed to say, her eyes reflecting the starlight. *I'm sorry if it is.*

We stepped once, twice, and three times into the woods. I glanced off to the right. I could see two trees, but nothing beyond. Then Arden said it, so low I could barely hear her: "Now."

I took off, my body weightless as it darted over downed tree limbs, through prickly brush, moving deeper into the charred wood. I kept my arms outstretched in the dark, feeling my way through it.

"You little—" Fletcher called out behind us, his

heavy boots clomping down in the clearing. "I'll cut your throats!"

Lark and Arden ran across the woods, splitting up somewhere in the blackness. Then the first gunshot rocked the air, quieting the birds and insects. I fell to the ground, scared Arden would cry out, but there was only the sound of footsteps, twigs snapping, and Fletcher's loud, raspy breaths behind me. I kept moving, crawling over the tangled brush, but Fletcher was getting closer. His shadow weaved in and out of the trees, moving steadily forward.

I struggled to my feet, my ankle twisting. There, beyond the charred forest, a light in the window of a house winked at me. I could just decipher the front porch, the tar roof a solid block against the shaded landscape.

"Get back here," he growled.

My pulse throbbed in my fingers and my toes. I ran toward the light, my chest heaving now, my legs tiring. *Keep going*, I told myself. *Just keep going.*

Soon the trees ended and the land folded out before me, a thick expanse of wildflowers. The light was much farther off than I thought—a hundred yards away, set beneath the towering sand sculptures.

Fletcher's boots hit rock as he stomped through the woods, his yells angrier than before. "You disgusting sow," he called out. "You think you can fool me."

I looked around. The giant cliffs rose off to my left, their backs turned on me. A sand road snaked along to my right. More woods spilled out in front of me, but even a sprint could not close the gap before Fletcher reached me. I had no cover except the thick blanket of flowers, their delicate blooms no more than a few inches wide.

I fell to the ground. The blue and gold buds crushed beneath my fingers. I turned on my side, pulling the stalks closer to hide me. When I lifted my head only slightly, I caught a glimpse of Fletcher at the edge of the trees, blood dripping from a gash on his forehead.

He turned, spitting into the dirt. "Come out, come out, wherever you are." He cocked his gun, raising the fine hairs on my arms.

As he made his way through the field, I sunk farther into the ground, wishing it would open up and swallow me whole. He moved slowly, the flowers parting at his knees, the mouth of the gun searching the length of the clearing. With each step his black boots crushed the blooms. When he was a couple yards away he squinted at me. He tilted his head to the side, as if he wasn't sure if I was a shadow or not.

I froze, not daring to breathe. My fingers dug into the

dirt, hard twigs and rocks scattering beneath me. Sweat beaded on my back. The air was trapped in my chest.

After careful consideration he turned and started away from me.

I closed my eyes, thankful he hadn't seen me, thankful that at the very least Lark and Arden had gotten an extra minute to run away. I relaxed back into the flowers, my lungs releasing my breath, when a thin branch broke under me. *Crack!*

Fletcher spun around. "Hello, babydoll."

I was up before he could properly aim the gun. The first shot went past me and I ran, my heart banging in my rib cage. Wind rushed past my ears. Another shot went off, splintering a tree in the distance. I kept running and didn't look back as the gun fired again. This time there was no shot, only the metallic click of the trigger. When I turned he was knocking the jammed gun on his hand.

I sprinted through the flowers, but he picked up his pace. His footsteps were faster than before, his body releasing short grunts of exertion.

"It's over," he said as he paused to fire.

I turned just in time to see him raise the gun, aiming it at my back. I squeezed my eyes shut and prayed that it would be quick, that my body wouldn't buck the way the deer's had, that I would leave this place without so much pain.

The shot sounded.

I felt my chest, waiting for the blood to gush from the wound, to feel the burning sensation of a bullet burrowing into my flesh. But there was nothing. No hole, no pain.

Nothing.

Behind me, Fletcher froze in place. He dropped his gun by his side. In the middle of his shirt a red stain slowly and determinedly spread outward, working its way to his sides and down his front. He made a gurgling sound and then fell—his mouth open—into the flowers.

I turned, my eyes resting on a figure across the field. An old woman came toward me. She looked nearly seventy, her ghostly white hair in a braid down her back. She petted the rifle in her hand like it was a dear pet.

"You all right?" she asked, studying my face. I kept my hand on my chest, steadied by my still-beating heart.

"Yes," I managed. "I think so."

She grabbed Fletcher's gun off the ground and emptied the ammunition into her hand. Then she kicked him, hard, in the side. He didn't move. He was already dead.

"Thank you," I whispered, not knowing if that was

the right thing to say.

The old woman smiled, her face beautifully lined. "Marjorie Cross," she said, holding out her wrinkled hand. "The pleasure is all mine."

twenty-five

"HERE WE ARE," MARJORIE SAID, PUSHING INTO THE house. "Go on now, settle yourselves down." She gestured to the living room, where a pink couch sat in front of the fire, yellowed lace covering each arm. A pot simmered in front of it, making the whole room smell of wild berries.

I waved Arden and Lark in behind me. "It's all right," I whispered, as Marjorie set the guns on the kitchen table. "We're safe."

"Otis!" Marjorie called up a set of stairs. "Otis!" She held her throat as she yelled, each word strained. "Sorry," she said, looking at us. "No place to buy hearing aids these days. You understand."

"Tell me why we're in this crazy lady's house?" Arden whispered as we sat down on the couch. She pressed at the side of her arm, where a scrape ran from her shoulder to her elbow, its pink insides dotted with ash.

"This *crazy lady* just saved my life." I'd called into the woods for twenty minutes before Arden and Lark finally showed themselves. They'd been afraid it was a trap, designed by Fletcher. Following Marjorie's lead, we'd made our way to the shingled house nestled into the woods, with only a lantern glowing in the window. It was the same light I'd seen when I was running from Fletcher.

Marjorie banged through the kitchen, stacking plates in one hand.

"It's pretty in here," Lark said. Her face was still wet, her jumper spotted with patches of red mud. "I like it."

The couch looked comfortable and the dainty pillows didn't smell of mildew, the way most post-plague cushions did. Delicate teacups—none of them chipped—and figurines of porcelain children locked together in a dance, or peering through the end of a telescope, filled a cabinet. The long wood dining table sat on the other side of the kitchen counter, decorated with a silver bowl of red, yellow, and green tomatoes.

I thought of the most coveted book in the library,

about a little girl named Nancy, who had tutus and bar-rettes and all the other luxuries we didn't have at School. When we were little, Pip, Ruby, and I used to curl up in bed together, reading about her family going to an ice cream shop, stopping on the part where she dresses her parents up, putting glasses on her father and a scarf on her mother. It was her house that I'd always loved, the giant sofa they collapsed into, the plants spotting the tables, the dresser that seemed always to be overflowing with clothes and toys. It was a real *home*, with painted walls and matching furniture. Like this.

The brick fireplace was studded with framed photos. A black-and-white portrait showed a baby girl in a checked pinafore. Another was of a boy in a white suit with a flower through the lapel. Then there was a photo of a young couple in high-waisted pants, their arms threaded through each other's. The blond woman, just older than I was, held the man's side, her hand over his heart.

I thought immediately of Caleb. He was out there somewhere, believing what he did. He was holding me in his memory, the way I shook his hand from my arm, my uncertainty when he'd asked me about Leif. He was out there without me.

"I see we have visitors." A silver-haired man climbed

down the stairs, heaving one leg with great effort. He was even older than Marjorie, his flannel shirt tucked loosely into his pants, which were white at the knees, the tan fabric worn from overuse. Lark startled at the sight of him, and I realized that a few weeks ago, I would have done the same. After so much time with Caleb—riding behind him on his horse or walking beside him in the woods—I didn't scare the way I once did.

Marjorie knelt down by the fire and scooped a spoonful of berries onto each plate. "I found them in the woods. Some savage was trying to kill them." She stared at Otis a moment too long. I sensed something had gone unspoken.

"What were you doing out there?" Otis pulled a chair from the dining room, its legs scraping against the beaten wood floor, and sat down beside us.

Lark's eyes welled. "This man, Fletcher, captured us. He was taking us somewhere to be sold." As she said it, she tucked her thick black hair behind her ears, her fingers shaking.

"We're from the Schools," Arden added. "We escaped."

Marjorie passed me a plate of steaming berries and I breathed in the tangy smell. The china had tiny purple roses along the rim. It was a welcome contrast to the simple metal saucers we'd eaten off at School and the gouged wood bowls Caleb had given us in the dugout. "How long have you been on your own?" Marjorie asked.

"Four days," Lark said.

Marjorie pointed to Arden and me.

I swallowed the berries. "I'm not sure . . . a few weeks?"

"Yes," Marjorie said. "It's hard to keep track of time out here on your own." As she spoke her eyes darted back to Otis. "Where are you headed then?"

Arden glanced sideways at me and paused. I raised one shoulder in a slight shrug. It was dangerous to trust anyone out here, but Marjorie had just saved my life. "We were going to follow Route eighty, to the place called Califia," Arden said, poking at her food with her fork.

"Smart girls," Otis said. Now that he was sitting down, his pant legs came above his ankles, revealing a wooden right leg. I stared at the light grain, the crudely cut corner that formed the ankle, burying a wedge deep into the pocket of his shoe. It looked like it had been carved from a downed tree limb. "And how do you plan to get there?"

"We've lost the road now," I said. "I don't know."

Lark shoveled the berries into her mouth, starved.

Marjorie glanced one more time at Otis. Then she stood, walking slowly to the lantern in the window. She picked it up and blew out the candle. "I do."

My gaze fell on the shelves behind her, where a black metal radio sat, a handset perched on its side.

"The Trail," I said out loud, to no one in particular.

Otis pointed to the floor. "Yes, you're on it right now."

"What do you mean?" Arden asked. She dropped her plate to her lap, letting the fork clink against the china. I had told her about the Trail when we were in Paul's room, but in her fever she must've forgotten its name.

Marjorie stood before us, her wrinkled hands laced together. "This is a safe house, just one stop along the way to several different dugouts, and Califia. We help orphans escape the King's regime."

Lark stared at the candle in the lantern, the smoke twisting from its black wick. "But the troops. Don't they know you're here?" She folded her thin arms across her chest, hugging herself.

"They're always suspicious," Otis told her. "They come by with their Jeeps every so often, ask us questions or inspect the house. But without evidence of any wrong-doing, there's not much they can do. We have permission to live outside the City of Sand."

"Permission?" I asked. I had heard of Strays before, of course, but they were scavengers, directionless wanderers. I likened them to those who had been called "homeless" in the old books, not people who lived in houses—in homes—like this.

Otis pulled his pant leg down, covering the sliver of wooden leg. "It's a long process and not many choose to go through with it unless there's a definitive reason. But we're old, and there's not a demand for us in the City of Sand. For the most part they leave us be."

Lark bit the skin of her finger. The firelight had warmed her cheeks, bringing out the beauty in her round, soft face. "What would they do to you if they knew you were helping us?"

"They'd kill us," Marjorie said simply. She gazed into the burning logs. They crackled, their charred carcasses shifting in the fire. "The King doesn't tolerate opposition. There have been so many disappearances in the City. A citizen who was working for the Trail, a man called Wallace, accidentally told an informant about the mission. He was gone within a week. His wife said he was taken right from his bed, only God knows where."

My tongue curled in my mouth like a shriveled snake. I had dreamed so much of that place, the clean slate streets, the man-made beaches where women sat under umbrellas with their books. How had I believed those lies for so long?

"You'll stay with us for a few days," Otis said. "Then we'll move you to another safe house. You can tell them by the lantern in the window—if it's on, there's room for you."

Lark kept nibbling at her fingers, the skin peeled back until it bled. "But if we get caught, we'll be killed—you said it yourself."

Marjorie tucked a strand of thick white hair into her braid. The shadows flickered in the glow of the fire, her expression unchanged. "Almost two hundred years ago, Harriet Tubman led slaves to freedom. And when they told her they didn't think they could, when they said they were too afraid, she pointed a gun at them and said"— Marjorie mimed a weapon in her grasp—"Go forward or die."

Otis put his hand over Marjorie's, bringing the invisible gun down. Then he turned to us, narrowing his eyes. "All she's saying is there's no room for fear anymore. That's what the King's regime is built on: the assumption that we're all too afraid to live any other way."

I remembered that feeling when I was at the edge of the wall. As much as I knew, as much as I'd seen inside that horrid building across the lake, something held me back. I heard a chorus of students whispering about the dogs and the gangs in the wild. I heard the steady beat of Headmistress Burns's gnarled fingers against a table, as she urged me to take my vitamins. The Teachers added to the melody with their tirades about men, who could manipulate women with a simple smile. My past had come together at once, in a great seductive song, telling me not to go.

"I suppose you're tired," Marjorie finally said. "Let me show you to your room." As Otis collected the empty plates, she stood, leading us down the narrow wood stairs. Beneath the house was a basement filled with stacked chairs and boxes, a beat-up gray machine with a keyboard, and some water-stained newspapers.

I picked up the one on top of the pile—the *New York Times*. It showed a picture of a woman reaching over a barricade, her mouth open in a wail. *Amid Crisis, Barricades Split Up Families*, it read. Teacher had described that city, the plague striking whole apartment buildings, their doors padlocked shut to lock people inside.

"Here?" Arden asked, pointing to a tattered couch nestled in the corner.

But Marjorie moved to the other side of the room, swinging open the doors of a pantry. She pulled off can after can of food, finally removing the middle shelf.

"Actually," she said, pushing a cobweb aside, "here."

She lit a lantern and shone it into the secret room. Two sets of bunk beds lined the walls and a metal sink sat in the corner. The walls were unfinished dirt, the earth floor covered with a thin gray mat. It reminded me of the mudrooms in the boy's dugout. "It's better, in case the troops surprise us in the night. Around the corner, about a hundred yards back, there's a trapdoor leading into the backyard. There are towels in there, a few changes of clothes, and some shoes as well," she said, glancing down at our bare, dirty feet.

Arden climbed through the pantry, throwing herself on one of the bottom bunks. "It's actually pretty big," she said, as Lark followed her inside.

Lark traded her ripped jumper for a fresh nightgown before collapsing into the mattress, pulling the thin quilt over her legs. She rested her head on the flattened pillow, for the first time seeming calm, her expression softening as she readied for sleep.

My stomach was full from the berries and my heartbeat had slowed into a steady rhythm. We were still on the run, still in danger, but I didn't feel the same terror in my chest. I looked into Marjorie's kind, weathered face.

"Go on." She gestured again to the pantry. The smell

of fire clung to her clothes, its scent comforting in its familiarity. "You'll be safe here—I promise."

I couldn't help it any longer. I hugged her, relaxing into the warmth of her body. The Teachers had never touched us, with the exception of a quick hand on the back as they led us to dinner, or a firm tap on the shoulder when our gaze had drifted outside the window during class. I had begged Teacher Agnes once—that first year I was at School—to untangle my hair. I had shrieked, kicked, my tiny arms flailing as I banged the brush on the porcelain sink. She had stood there for over an hour, hands in her pockets, not moving until I worked at the knot myself.

Gradually Marjorie's arms left her sides and she wrapped them around me, too. My hands pressed against the hard bones in her back, feeling how tiny she was beneath her loose linen shirt. "Thank you," I said, repeating the phrase over and over, the words growing fainter each time. "Thank you, thank you."

twenty-six

WE AWOKE TO THE SMELL OF BAKED BREAD. "WE HAVE fresh eggs for you girls," Otis said, pulling out the chairs around the dining room table. I looked at the spread before us, the steaming scrambled eggs, the wild boar meat salted and dried into thin strips, the soft bread on the heated stone of Marjorie's oven. I smiled, my throat choked again with emotion.

"This looks delicious," I said. Lark sat down and piled a heaping spoonful onto her plate. She hadn't bothered changing out of her nightgown.

Arden looked around the room, taking in the front windows, the side windows, and the doors that faced the backyard. The curtains were all drawn tightly shut. "Are they vampires?" she whispered.

Marjorie moved around her kitchen, chopping tomatoes and throwing them into the bowl. I thought again of the chase through the woods, of Fletcher, and the wound that opened in his chest when she shot him.

"Is he still outside?" I asked, keeping my eyes on her.

Marjorie stopped chopping. Then she gestured to the front window with her knife. "Bill and Liza are taking care of him."

Arden stared at the plate of red meat. "Who are Bill and Liza?"

"Our cats," Marjorie said. She set the tomatoes down in front of Otis, her hand on his neck.

Lark swallowed, her eyes jumping from Marjorie to Otis and back. "Your *cats* are taking care of Fletcher?"

Otis nodded, then took another bite of his meat.

I pulled at the curtain on the front window, letting in a thin stream of white light that exposed the dust in the air. A hundred yards off, two mountain lions were tearing at Fletcher's carcass, their jaws plunging into his bloody flesh. One of the beasts held a hand in its mouth, the gray fingers sticking out between its teeth.

"Best not to go near the window, dear," Marjorie said,

summoning me back to the table. "There's always the chance the troops are watching."

Lark chewed on a strip of boar. She eyed Marjorie, then Otis, warily. "So you're . . . married?"

Marjorie ran her fingers over Otis's, her eyes dancing in amusement. "I met Otis long before the plague. I was living in New York at the time—"

"They don't know what New York is," Otis teased. Marjorie scrunched her nose at him, feigning annoyance. He turned to us, but his gaze was far off. "It was across the country, and it was one of the most spectacular cities in the world. Buildings that shot up from the ground, the sidewalks so packed with people you had to dart through them. Underground trains and hot dogs that you could buy on the street."

I had read books set in New York—*The Great Gatsby*, *The House of Mirth*—but it still sounded impossible. The sheer number of people it would take to fill a skyscraper, to fill a street . . . I hadn't seen that many people in my entire life.

Marjorie brought his hand to her lips and kissed it. "Thank you, darling. I was in New York and there he was one night, sitting across from me, telling some ridiculous story about recycling."

"It wasn't about recycling," Otis chuckled to himself. "But that's okay."

"What's recycling?" Arden asked.

"It doesn't matter. The point is," Marjorie continued, "I wasn't listening. I just kept watching him, and I thought: This man, this someone—I didn't even know his name—is so alive. He was the most exciting person I'd ever met . . . and the most familiar." Otis kissed Marjorie's hand.

I thought of the way Caleb looked at me, how I could feel each inch between us. The way the crescent shaped scar in his cheek crinkled when he smiled, how he always stared straight ahead when he was saying something important.

"I kept thinking he'd turn into a knucklehead, but every minute I spent with him, I just loved him more," Marjorie finished.

Arden swallowed a bite of eggs. "Is that why you didn't go, like everyone else?" she asked. "When the King called for the City of Sand, were they going to split you up?"

Marjorie looked down, her finger tracing the grain of the wood table. "The King doesn't want people like us in the City. We're too old to be of real use to him. We don't have any resources he could use. He wanted me to teach in the Schools, and they tried to make Otis work at the labor camps. But no, that's not why."

"We didn't go," Otis said, "because it was wrong. It still is."

"During the plague, and after, everyone was so afraid," Marjorie continued. "There was a formal government before it happened, a democracy. But the illness came on so fast, half of the country's leaders were dead within the first six months. The laws were irrelevant— no one was reading the Constitution. Information was withheld. Some of that was intentional, I'm certain now. For a long time, without electricity, without phones, we had no clue what was happening. Then this politician announces plans to rebuild. He was only supposed to be in power until things got settled, but it was two more years before the plague ended. By then everyone trusted him. They believed him when he said America needed to be unified under one leader. They were so afraid, they just listened and followed. They never questioned, and it only got worse."

"Maybe it will be different though, if we wait?" Lark's face rested in her hands. "It can't go on forever. Maybe once the City of Sand is built and—"

"'Time itself is neutral,'" Marjorie corrected, her words steady with the rhythm of memorization. "And 'we will have to repent in this generation not merely for the vitriolic words and actions of the bad people but for the appalling silence of the good people.'"

Otis leaned back in his chair, his bad leg lying straight before him. "Martin Luther King Jr."

"Who is that?" I asked, picking up the last piece of boar.

Otis and Marjorie looked at each other. "There's still a lot you girls need to know," he said.

"We have a few days," I answered. I had learned so much in School, but it all seemed worthless now. My real education had begun with Caleb. I felt as if I was only getting started; the truth was something I couldn't yet imagine.

"Yes," Marjorie said. "We do." She smoothed her hands over the table, her eyes meeting Otis's. "For now, how about you turn on the projector. I bet these girls have never even seen a proper movie."

Otis walked to the middle of the living room, where a flat box was connected to a giant pack covered in shiny gray tape. "Runs on D batteries," he said, smacking the top of it. "Figured it out myself." He pressed a few buttons and a white rectangle appeared on the wall above the fireplace.

"What is it?" Lark asked, sitting down on the couch. She pulled a lace pillow into her lap. Slow music filled the room and the wall above the fireplace flashed the word GHOST.

I'd only ever seen the small bits of video sometimes captured from beyond the wall. We would crowd around, staring at the tiny screen that the Teacher held in her hands. I'd seen packs of wild dogs feeding on deer. I'd seen tall grass moving as gangs made their way through it, crawling on their elbows and knees to avoid being seen. But this was entirely different. Shots flitted across the screen: a hammer breaking down a rickety old wall, a woman jumping into a man's arms for a kiss, people making their way down large city streets, just as Otis had described. Arden and I stood, staring.

"You can sit down." Marjorie laughed, ushering us to the couch. My body collapsed into the cushions and I slowly forgot where I was, instead disappearing into the world in front of me. I blushed when Sam wrapped his arms around Molly and the wet pottery collapsed beneath their fingers. My body tensed, my breaths shorter, as they were attacked on the dark street. By the end, I covered my mouth to keep from crying as they said good-bye.

When the wall went black, Lark begged Otis to put on

another. But I couldn't speak. The movie had been about love, about separation and death. I could only think of Caleb.

"I'm going to lie down," I said, careful not to meet Arden's gaze.

Marjorie stopped cutting. "Are you all right, dear?"

"Stay," Lark urged. "We'll just watch one more."

I was already at the basement stairs. "I'm fine, just feeling tired. It must be everything catching up to me," I lied. Arden gave me an understanding nod as I started down the steps.

"She sometimes gets like this," I heard her say over my shoulder. "It's nothing to worry about."

In the dark secret room I lay down on the bed and allowed myself to cry. Soon I was sobbing, the deep, choked sobs of someone who never got to say good-bye. There was only that bunk, only the road to Califia, just a few days until I was back on the run. I would never see Caleb again.

When Lark and Arden came to bed hours later, stacking the cans behind them, I pretended to sleep. Arden pulled the blanket over my bare toes and carefully tucked it around my feet. "Good night," she whispered. Soon their breaths were softer, slower, and they fell into a deep slumber.

I would not sleep, though—I couldn't. I thought of the wood shelf that lined Marjorie's wall, of the radio that sat on top of it. I imagined Caleb that night at the labor camp, twisting the knob of the machine back and forth, listening to it as he lay in bed. I remembered the one that sat on that tiny broken table in his room. He had to listen to it still. How else would he receive word from the City? How else would he communicate with Moss?

I stood, not feeling the hours that had passed, the exhaustion of the journey with Fletcher, or the tears that had emptied me. Unstacking the cans as quietly as I could, I felt only possibility.

He especially loved people—is so happy, especially remembering Eloise.

Upstairs the living room was dark. I felt around, eventually finding a lantern on the kitchen table. I thought of getting Marjorie, but there was too much to tell. About the raid, what happened with Leif, and the sentence that had sent Caleb running into the woods.

I opened the kitchen cabinets, looking past burnt pots and jars of food, for a piece of paper with a location on it.

Teacher had said once, long ago, that before the plague a whole system existed for dispersing mail. Addresses, was the word she had used. I searched a drawer of utensils, and another of batteries, rubber bands, and scissors. In the table behind the sofa there were old photos of a young Marjorie, pregnant, with a small daughter clinging to her leg. I flipped to another of two children in a soapy bath. It was strange that they hadn't mentioned their daughters, that the walls hadn't revealed even a trace of them.

Beneath more photos sat three thick paper cards with pictures on them. One said *Phuket, Thailand*, with water stretching to the horizon. The back read: *Hi Mom and Dad, Thom and I are having a great time. The most beautiful beaches in the world are here. It's paradise. Love, Libby.* The address beside it read *Sedona, Arizona*.

I pulled the radio down from the shelf, twisting its knob the same way I'd seen the Teachers do at School, during our assemblies. A low static filled the room. I held the handset in my palm and pressed on the button. The static stopped. I spoke carefully, making sure each word was clear. "If the islands south ever vanish, even farther into navy depths, my Eloise could appreciate lovely endless blues." I repeated it again, then another time, as if I were telling him simple truths: I missed him.

I needed him. I was sorry.

After I'd said it ten times, the rhythm overtaking me, I added, "See Eloise dive over nimbly, ambitiously." I repeated that. Then I released the button. There was only static.

Please, say something, I thought, imagining him in that beaten armchair, my voice filling his room. *Say something.* But only the dumb rush of nothingness hit my ears. I waited there, staring at the black handset, until finally I set it back on the shelf. He might not have heard. He might still be angry. And yet I wasn't deterred.

Tomorrow, and the next day, and every day until we left I would send out more messages. My voice would echo in that cavern, the words wound together in coded sentences, recited over and over until they reached him, there in the night.

twenty-seven

"I WANT TO WATCH MORE MOVIES," LARK SAID. SHE dropped the plates, crusted with the remnants of our breakfast, into the sink. Marjorie and Otis sat at one end of the table finishing their tea, while Arden and I played rummy.

"No more movies." Arden looked at me over the cards fanned out in her hand. Her normally messy black bob was combed straight behind her ears, and her skin, scrubbed clean, had a healthy glow. "We don't need to see any more tortured love stories."

I tugged at the frayed ends of my hair, my mind half there and half with Caleb. After sending out the message last night I'd collapsed into the worn mattress, letting my body sink deeply into sleep. Soon my thoughts gave way to dreams, and I saw him in his room, his hands resting on his radio.

I saw him listening to the message.

Lark started over to the table, pointing a finger at Arden. The sweater she wore was three sizes too big and fell down over her bare shoulder. "You're not the only one who gets to decide. I might be younger than you, but I have a vote—"

"All right, all right," Otis said, throwing up his hands. He laughed, his gray eyes meeting Marjorie's. "It feels like old times."

I remembered the picture of the beach and the scrawled note from the girl named Libby. "Do you have a daughter?" I asked, setting my cards facedown in front of me.

"Two," Marjorie said. She wiped off the table, scraping at a dried tomato seed with her fingernail. "Libby and Anne."

Otis stood. His back faced us as he dumped a bucket of water into the sink. "They were what you hope for when you have children," he said. "They were twenty-seven and thirty-three." When he turned back he had tears in his eyes.

"We don't talk much about that anymore, though," Marjorie offered. The dishes clinked together in the sink.

"Anyway, Otis just meant that it's good to have you girls here."

I thought of my own mother and the letter she had written me. She had tucked it into my pocket on the day that the trucks came—the last thing I'd ever have of her. It was lost now, back with my other keepsakes at the dugout, never to be held again. I thought about how she had snuggled next to me in my bed, reading me stories about a talking elephant named Babar. She had tied my shoelaces, dressed me, and combed my hair. *I love you*, she said silently, with every button she buttoned, every wrinkle she pressed flat. *I love you, I love you, I love you.*

"We're happy to be here, too," I said.

But Marjorie was looking at something over my shoulder. The lines on her face seemed deeper, more severe, as she walked to the bookshelves. Her hand touched first the top shelf, then the black metal radio beneath it. "Someone moved the radio."

The way she said it—slow, tinged with anger—scared me. Otis rested his arms on the counter, his gaze settling on Lark.

"Why are you looking at me?" Lark said. She wheeled backward, pulling her sweater tight around her shoulders. "I didn't do anything."

"I did," I said, the breaths tightening in my chest.

Marjorie tilted her head, studying me. "What did you do?" she asked, her voice louder than usual.

Arden turned to me now too, a look of confusion on her pale face. She set down her cards.

"I had to send out a message to someone—but it was in code."

"What code did you use?" Marjorie said urgently, coming toward me. She twisted the end of her purple scarf until it was a hard, tight coil.

Arden gripped my arm. "To Caleb?" she asked.

"Who the hell is Caleb?" Otis asked. I flinched, my breath quickening.

Marjorie circled the table to reach me. "It doesn't matter who he was," she said, squeezing her fingers into my shoulder. "It matters what code she used. Now tell me, which one was it?"

Marjorie and Arden stared at me, their eyes pleading and urgent. I stood, backing against the wall. "The code—the only one."

Marjorie slapped her hand onto the table, sending her glass toppling over, water running to the floor. "There isn't only one. There have been thirty different codes since the Trail started five years ago."

The room grew too hot. My body slicked with a thin layer of sweat. I could barely make out the words. "He especially loved people—"

"No!" Otis cried, pounding his fist on the counter. "No, no, no!"

Lark's eyes welled. "What? What's wrong?"

"It has to be some mistake," Arden said hastily. "Maybe she didn't do it right, maybe it never went out. Who would listen to it anyway?"

"Everyone," Otis snapped. "Everyone—that's who."

Marjorie was rubbing at her forehead. The sunlight glowed through the curtains, making her skin look pink. Finally, she turned to Otis. "Get the bags. We don't have much time."

"I'm sorry," I said, feeling my throat constrict.

Outside something sounded in the distance. Everyone froze. Through the chorus of birds and wind, I heard something foreign, something terrifying: the steady roar of an automobile engine.

Marjorie went to the window, pulling back a fingerful of curtain. "They're already here."

"Who?" Lark asked, biting her lip nervously.

Otis opened a cabinet above the counter, feeling around behind some glass jars. He pulled down a handgun and tucked it into the belt of his pants. "The troops."

Marjorie ran to the sink, pulling three of the five soaking dishes out and throwing them, with a clatter, into a lower cabinet. She plunged her fingers in the soapy water, searching for the extra forks and knives, but Otis pushed her away. "Don't—" he directed. "Just go."

Her arms were soaked to the elbows, white suds clinging to her skin. "Follow me," she finally said, starting down the stairs. Lark reached for the tail of Marjorie's shirt, her cheeks now wet with tears.

"What did you say?" Arden asked. She grabbed my hand as we raced down the stairs. "What did you say in the message?"

The engine grew louder as the troops approached the house. Tires crunched across the yard. I opened my mouth, but I couldn't tell her that I had relayed, in great detail, who I was and where I was. I couldn't tell her I'd snuck up into the living room at night and risked all of our lives.

In the basement, Marjorie threw open the cabinet's wood doors. "Help me," she pleaded, sweeping the cans off the shelf in one great motion. They fell to the cement floor, their corners dented.

Arden yanked the shelf out and Lark and I ran inside the secret room. Arden came in fast behind us.

"Don't say a word," Marjorie whispered as she re-stacked the cans on the shelf.

Upstairs, the front door banged open and male voices, deep and gruff, demanded something.

"Hurry," Lark cried, her fingers tapping on the wood shelf. "Please Marjorie, hurry."

Marjorie bent over and collected the cans in her arms, putting them back onto the shelf. Her wrinkled hands moved slowly, revealing her age. "I'm going as fast as I can," she said, her voice quaking. "I'm going." She wiped at her face. I realized, then, she was crying. Thin streams ran along the lines of her face.

The voices grew louder. The sound of boots crashed overhead, sending tiny pieces of plaster raining down on us.

"Just my wife," Otis said, then more footsteps. Marjorie was cradling the last of the cans when the soldiers, clad in green and brown, appeared on the stairs. Arden squeezed my hand, pulling me deeper into the room.

I pressed my other hand against Lark's trembling mouth, trying to silence her. The glass doors of the pantry fell closed. Through the spaces in the stacked cans we could make out parts of the room. We stood there, in the shadows, watching as the men came down the stairs.

In an instant, Marjorie straightened—her face stiffened and her hands relaxed by her sides. "What can I do for you this time, gentlemen? Lieutenant Calverton," she said, acknowledging the older soldier, who had a crooked nose and hair streaked with silver. Beside him, a slender man with pale skin kept his hand on his gun. "Sergeant Richards. You've come to harass us again?"

They stood at the bottom of the steps, both clean-shaven, their faces taut and shiny. "Enough games, Marjorie," Calverton said. "We know you're hiding a girl named Eve here. She's the property of the King."

Arden pulled me closer. My legs were wobbly beneath me, but Arden gripped my side, holding me up. "We're doing no such thing," Otis said. "When will you leave us alone? We're just trying to survive, like everyone else."

Richards worked his way through the cardboard boxes, ripping them open and peering inside. He stomped through the cellar, opening a door beneath the staircase, patting down the tattered couch, and rapping on the walls behind a pile of old machines. "Do we have to go through this every time?" Marjorie asked, crossing her arms.

Otis came down the last steps on his bad leg. He leaned

against the wall, his arm clutched to his side, concealing the gun beneath his elbow. "You won't find anything," he said, his breaths short.

"Something tells me you're lying," Calverton said. Then he pointed to the cupboard doors. My heart kept on, its steady rhythm reminding me that for now, I was still alive. Arden pushed me down behind the bunk beds, then pulled Lark close. We huddled together, slowing our breaths to quiet them, as the younger soldier opened the doors.

From behind the bars of the bunks I could see his legs. I could hear the cans clinking together on the top shelf. He moved down, over the second shelf, sliding against the wood. Then the cans covering the passageway moved. Lark whimpered as light poured into the narrow room. I looked up, my eyes locking with the soldier's.

"Sir," he said, pushing more cans aside. "Sir, there are more sows—"

Otis grabbed the gun from his belt and fired it into Richard's side. The soldier fell, pulling the shelf on top of him. He clutched at his shoulder, where the bullet had ripped through his shirt.

As Otis threw himself into Calverton, Marjorie turned to us. "Go!" she yelled, pointing behind us to the tunnel that snaked into darkness. "Now!"

Calverton slammed Otis into the wall, knocking the weapon from his grasp. He wiped off his uniform where Otis had grabbed him, smoothing down the puckered cloth. Then he lowered his gun.

"No! Stop!" Marjorie yelled. Her hands reached out, strained, trying to close the gap between them. It happened too fast. One shot, then another, burying themselves in Otis's chest. He was dead before he hit the ground.

Lark rushed into the tunnel and Arden followed, dragging me behind. But my feet were heavy, sadness already overtaking me. I kept my head turned, watching as Marjorie kneed the soldier, hard, in the side. It barely slowed him down. He raised his gun again and struck Marjorie across her cheek. She fell on top of Otis, her arms holding him still, as the soldier lowered his gun again and fired one last blast.

twenty-eight

ARDEN TUGGED AT MY ARM, BUT I STOOD FROZEN, watching the scene as if it were playing on the wall above the fireplace. Richards squeezing his eyes in pain, the spatter of blood against his pale cheek, Marjorie slumped over, her white braid slowly turning red.

Calverton lunged toward us, but I couldn't move. After a moment, Arden yanked me hard, sending me stumbling forward.

We ran through the tunnel, our steps pounding out a constant rhythm as we traveled farther into the blackness. My mind felt clouded from the unreality of it all. Marjorie and Otis had been shot. They were dead. It was my fault. As much as I repeated these facts, they didn't make any sense.

When we finally reached the end of the tunnel, we hit a set of stairs. A thin strip of light streamed in from a long crack in the ceiling. Lark threw herself up against the trapdoor, but the metal didn't give. "It's stuck," she cried, beating on it with her fists. Finally the door raised an inch, revealing a thick tree branch that had fallen over it, barring it shut.

Behind us, cans clinked together as the soldier plunged through the cabinet. Lark stepped back into the darkness, letting us wedge our way between the stairs and the door. The soldiers were just around the corner when a shot sounded.

"Don't fire at her—we need her alive!" Calverton yelled.

"Push harder!" Arden cried, pressing her palms to the door.

"Stop! By order of the King of the New America!" Richards's voice called through the tunnel.

Arden and I rushed at the door again, throwing our hands against it so hard it hurt. In one gratifying crack the branch broke, the bark splintering down on us as the doors flung apart, revealing the white morning light.

Arden sprang into the open air. I paused on the steps, turning quickly to help Lark. But she was slumped at the bottom of the stairs. Blood slicked her hair and pooled, a purplish red, around her skull.

"No!" I reached down and grabbed her, feeling the warmth of the puddle through my shoes. The shot had buried itself in the back of her neck. "Lark!"

"We have to go," Arden said from up above. She pointed to the woods. "I don't want to but we—"

Before she could finish, the soldiers turned the corner, their guns raised. Richards's arm was bandaged with Marjorie's purple scarf.

I ran furiously beside Arden, kicking the metal door shut behind me, Lark's body locked beneath it. The sun was unforgiving, beating on the scorched lawn and lightening the shadows beneath the charred trees. Giant red rocks spread out over the landscape, creating an impenetrable wall. The shrubs were shorter, the sand hot, the next house a tiny square on the horizon. Even outside, there was nowhere to hide.

The door clattered open behind us. Calverton moved steadily across the grass as he reloaded his gun.

"Come on," I said, darting right, away from the charred forest we had come through that night with Fletcher. We made our way in and out of the trees, the thick shrubs ripping at my calves. Far beyond Marjorie's house, over dunes and past the tree line, a cracked road opened into a neighborhood.

A bullet hit a tree in front of Arden, burrowing into the wood. "They're trying to kill me," she yelled, as she jumped a rotten log. I kept running, and for a moment the soldiers disappeared behind a stretch of tall brush.

"There," I said, pointing to a house overgrown with grass. We took off behind it, pushing through the battered gate.

In the middle of the yard was an empty pool, the skeleton of a dog resting at its bottom. Lining the house was a collapsed deck with overturned chairs. A wood shack sat in the corner, its white paint peeling off in sheets. Surrounding all of it, nearly eight feet high, stood a yellow fence.

Arden ran at it, landing her heel into its side. It wouldn't give. Beyond the gate the soldiers' steps drew nearer. Arden kicked the fence again, turning her foot to the side, putting all her weight into it. Her eyes watered from the effort. "No, this can't be happening. No!"

There was no entrance or exit around the other side of the house. There were no breaks in the wall, nothing we could use to climb. Only one way in and one way out.

"We're trapped." My hands shook with the realization.

Arden pulled me around the shack. We crouched low, her hand slippery inside mine, as we watched through its broken window. The soldiers came in, their guns drawn, and circled the pool. Calverton raised his finger to his mouth, as if to say *Shhhh*.

"I'm sorry," I whispered into Arden's ear, my words barely audible. I had sent out the message, calling the soldiers to Marjorie's house. Now I had led us to our capture. I had chosen the wrong way.

Richards pulled a flashlight from his belt and searched under the broken deck. Arden's eyes locked on the overturned chairs, stacked together near the back door of the house. She pointed to them. "You can use one to get over. You'll go out the back."

I watched Calverton through the broken glass. He went around the other side of the shack, to where an old doghouse sat.

"What about you?" I asked, already knowing the answer.

Arden tried to smile but her face looked strained. "I'll distract them. Don't worry—I'll meet you in Califia," she said. "I'll find the road again."

"No," I said, wiping at my eyes. I wanted to believe her, but I knew how impossible it would be, for either of us, to make it on our own. "You can't. I'd rather be taken to the City, I don't care, just don't—"

"You would do the same for me," she interrupted. "You already did."

She didn't wait for me to respond. She slipped her hand from mine and darted out into the yard. Richards sprang up from his position at the deck and chased her, Calverton following close behind. They kept running, their backs disappearing beyond the gate.

Gunshots broke the silence. I waited, scared I'd hear Arden scream. But there was only the soldier's voice, moving farther out, and heavy footsteps pounding the dry earth.

I started toward the fence, pulling the chair to it as Arden had instructed. I imagined her there, her hand on my arm, guiding me over. I ran in the opposite direction, imagining the blue shock of her sweater winding through the trees. Sometimes I saw her turn to me, her cheeks flushed red, or nod off to a trail, signaling for us to change direction. I kept going, the massive rocks behind me, cutting into the sky. It wasn't until the air cooled and the woods dimmed that I stopped, and realized I was completely alone.

twenty-nine

TIME PASSED. TWO DAYS, MAYBE THREE. I HAD NO REA-
son to count.

I lay in the brown-ringed bathtub of an abandoned
house, holding a dull knife. My feet were bloodied and
bare. I'd run so far my laces had broken and I'd lost my
shoes somewhere along the way.

Drifting in and out of sleep, I pictured the cellar: Otis
and Marjorie, their bodies in a tangled, writhing heap.
Lark's face pressed into the cold cement floor. The smell of
gunpowder and blood. Calverton pausing to wipe a scuff
from his boot. Arden's fingers digging desperately into my
arm. Richards's eyes, gray and unfeeling, meeting mine.

It should've been the first thing I said when I awoke. It should've been a priority to tell of the message, of the way I'd used the radio. Instead, I'd buzzed happily on the thrill of the dream, on that silly fantasy of Caleb in his room.

I wondered if there was something inside me that was rotten. I had left Pip. I had left Pip and Ruby and Marjorie and Otis and Lark, moving swiftly forward, their lives in my horrible wake. I didn't want to witness any of it anymore, the boarded-up homes and the tattered red flags hanging from cracked windows, PLAGUE printed across them in black. The children were too young to be motherless. I wished to no longer hear the grayed bones crunching underneath the brush or feel the now inexorable fear that seemed to work its way inside my rib cage, rocking me at my core.

There was no desire to eat, no desire to move. I hadn't drunk anything in days. My legs were frail and my back burned. As the sun slipped below the window ledge I dropped the knife, knowing that if I stayed there in that tub, the end would come before the troops did.

The warmth of the day vanished. Hours came, hours went. In the moments between unconsciousness, I was with Arden, behind the shack. I had the sudden vision of her face in the light, her words: *You would do the same for me.* That memory gave way to one of my mother standing at the doorway as she watched me loaded onto the truck. I saw the plate of eggs that Marjorie slid in front of me, felt the way Arden had tucked my toes beneath the blanket, Otis's wrinkled hand covering my own.

My body curled and seized, ridden with shame. In School and out of School, I had believed that love was a liability—something that could be wielded against you. I began to weep, finally knowing the truth: love was death's only adversary, the only thing powerful enough to combat its clawing, desperate grasp.

I would not remain there. I would not give in. If only for Arden, if only for Marjorie and Otis, if only for my mother. *I love you, I love you, I love you.*

I heaved myself out of the tub. I was weak. The house was now dim. Broken tiles cut at my feet. The rotted floorboards threatened more splinters. Bile caked the front of my tattered gray sweater. I didn't care. I searched each room, moving with slow determination. I found a dented tin beneath the refrigerator and kept going through cupboards and drawers. I ran my hand over bookshelves until I discovered what it was I'd been looking for.

The atlas was like the one Teacher Florence had shown us our eleventh year of School, its edges bound with leather. I studied the pages, looking at meaningless green stretches of land. I flipped over maps of strange places with names like Tonga, Afghanistan, El Salvador. There was so much of the world I'd never known about. I wondered what those places looked like, if they were vast stretches of land or peaked with mountains or perhaps lush, tropical paradises. Had they all been ravaged by the plague as we had?

Turning page after page, nothing resembled anything I recognized. On the shelf beside it was another one, thinner. In it lines crisscrossed the maps, each one dotted with a number. I finally found it: Route 80. My finger traced it all the way across the page, to where it met a blue mass. The ocean.

For the first time in days, my terror gave way to possibility. I studied the maps, ripping out the pages that said Sedona, Arizona, the green area below Route 80, and the places called Los Angeles and San Francisco. I pieced it all together on the floor, locating the giant lake Caleb had lived on—Tahoe.

Tomorrow morning I would scavenge supplies and

go north toward Califia. I couldn't stay another day in the house, just waiting to die. Even if the troops found me, even if I collapsed out in the desert, in the shadow of those great rocks, I had to move. I had to at least try.

 thirty

I SET OUT EARLY, BEFORE THE BIRDS AWOKE. I FOUND A
rusted tin of peas, and ate half for dinner and half for
breakfast, drinking the last of the congealed liquid inside.
Moving from house to house, scouring the neighborhood,
I discovered two more unlabeled cans and a jar of jam.
It wasn't much, but it would be enough to take me a few
days, until I found another place safe enough to rest.

The morning was cold as I moved north, through the
short shrubs beside the roads. I pulled my sweater close
to me, grateful to whoever had lived in that house. They'd
left a few changes of clothes and a pair of size eight sneakers, NIKE written across the sides. The map directed me

over more desert, to where land stretched out a golden brown. I walked as fast as I could, my legs still weak, stopping every hour to take a fingerful of jam, the sweet sugary rush providing more fuel.

Just before noon I reached an intersection. Rusted cars filled a large parking lot, and across from it stood a brick building with broken windows, BANK OF AMERICA written on its front in red.

I was walking toward a ransacked supermarket when I heard a strange sound. My body recognized it before my memory did: a car's engine. I darted through the broken front door of the bank and inside, where desks lined the windows. I crawled underneath and waited.

The car drove slowly down the street. From my hiding place I could hear the familiar roar, the crunching sound of garbage breaking under its weight. My hands shook when the car paused, puttering for a moment as if taking one long, dreadful breath. Then it started on its way again.

When the sound finally disappeared I rested against the desk, my body renewed with purpose. The troops were looking for me again. I had to keep moving.

Heading for the door, I stepped on a pile of green papers strewn across the tiled floor, covered in sand and dust. I picked one up that read 100, an old man's stern face on it, realizing, suddenly, that it was a piece of old money. I crumpled the bill and threw it down, leaving it in the dust once more.

I moved quickly, past the stone backs of stores and markets, the Dumpsters behind them filled with bones. I kept running, running, until I was away from the broken stoplights and the shells of cars overturned on the side of the street. The cramped town opened up into desert.

The flat terrain stretched out in front of me, with only short bushes on the side of the road, hardly enough for cover. I stripped down to my yellowed T-shirt to camouflage me against the dry, cracked dirt. Checking the map one last time, I started across the plain, toward a cluster of houses in the distance. The red rocks climbed up to the sky, the clouds brushing past every so often. There was no sign of the Jeep. *The houses can't be too far,* I thought to myself. *Just go. Don't look back.*

The sun peeked over the horizon, warming my skin. I tried to imagine Arden there, or Pip kicking up dirt as she hummed a song, but their ghosts never appeared.

I took another scoop of jam, letting the bitter raspberry seeds pop beneath my teeth. It spurred me forward, the pack lighter on my back, my steps faster as I kept on toward the houses and certain cover. The windows, the doors, the playground in the yard, slowly came into view.

Then I heard the engine again. It must have stopped on the road behind me, waiting. I sprinted, pumping my arms as hard as I could. I cut across the broken pavement, to where the brush was thicker.

But the car sped up. I could hear it after me, gaining, closing in. I pumped my arms faster, my rubber soles beating the pavement, but it was no use. There was the sound of the car slowing, then stopping, the door opening, and footsteps padding on the road. My legs burned with the effort. My body slowed, but I kept pushing. I didn't want to be caught like this, out in the desert. Not now, not after how far I'd come.

"Stop! Stop!"

Tears trailed down my face, cutting through the thin layer of dust that coated my skin.

"Eve!" The man's voice yelled again, but I didn't turn back. Then his hand gripped my arm, pulling me down into the thick brush. I didn't struggle. My limbs went numb as the brute turned me over onto my back. I covered my face.

"Eve," the voice said again, softer. "It's me."

I opened my eyes to the face I'd imagined so many

times. Caleb smiled, his hair tickling my forehead. I pressed my hands to his cheeks, wondering if I was having a waking dream. His skin was firm against my fingers. I wasn't sure whether to cry or laugh.

Instead I just hugged him. Our bodies pressed into one; our arms pulled the other nearer and nearer still, until nothing was between us, not even air.

"You heard my message?" I finally asked.

Caleb lifted his head. "I wanted to reply, but I couldn't. I knew the troops were listening and were already on their way. It was the code from—"

"I know," I said, wiping at my eyes. "It was the wrong one."

"We have to go," Caleb said, helping me out of the dirt. A rusted red car sat on the road, puttering on the pavement. "They're still searching for you." We started toward the car, a boxy thing with VOLVO written across the front. Thick yellow foam billowed out of a gash in the front seat.

As Caleb pressed a pedal beneath the wheel, my body relaxed into the cushion. The ache in my legs subsided. Behind us, the dust blew up, and the world disappeared into a perfect blanket of orange.

thirty-one

AIR BLEW IN THE WINDOW, RUSHING OVER MY SKIN AND tangling my hair. Golden dust coated Caleb's face, his brown dreadlocks, even the soft skin behind his ears. "How did you find me?" I asked.

We rode over a shallow hole and the car lurched sideways. "There's only one stop on the Trail in Sedona."

"So you were at the house. You went in the cellar?" I dug my fingers into the ripped cushion. The backseat was strewn with clothes, rusted, unmarked cans, and two mud-caked knapsacks.

Caleb nodded, his gaze meeting mine for a brief moment.

My throat closed. I had seen the soldier lower his gun, I had seen him aim. But I had to ask anyway. "And Marjorie . . . was she . . ."

"They were gone. Three of them." Caleb rested his hand on my arm. His T-shirt was split at the seams, revealing a patch of sunburnt shoulder. "There was blood leading out the trapdoor, from the house. I followed it to the woods but I lost it a mile in and I was certain," he paused, adjusting his seat belt, "that they had captured you. I was about to turn back when I saw something on the ground—a woman's shoe. I found the other one a hundred yards north and kept going in that direction, searching the sides of the road."

"Did you see Arden?" My hand pressed against my chest, steadying my heart. "She saved me. She left to distract the soldiers."

Caleb rubbed his finger on the wheel, working at some invisible spot. He paused, then shook his head. "I didn't."

I wiped at my eyes. "She said she'll meet me at Califia, but . . . she's on her own now and I—" I broke off, thinking of her somewhere in the wild, her pale skin blistered in the heat, miles still from the road. Or worse, in the backseat of a Jeep, the property of the soldiers, being taken back to School.

Caleb squeezed my arm. "She's tough. As long as she stays hidden, she'll be okay."

We turned in to a broken town, the sun disappearing behind the distant hills. Cracks zigzagged along the pavement, rattling the green coins piled in the car's console. The vehicle, beaten and weathered, kept going, and I felt safer with each mile that brought us closer to Califia.

"About Leif," I started. Caleb held the map over the steering wheel, its corners pressed under his palms. We sped past empty storefronts and knots of brown, shriveled shrubs. "It wasn't . . ."

"I know," Caleb said quickly. "You don't need to explain." He set the map down and looked into my eyes. His lips were red from too much sun.

"I didn't know if I'd ever see you again." My voice cracked as I said it. "You shouldn't have—"

"I wish I hadn't run away," Caleb replied, his voice louder than before. He slowed the car and turned to me. His green eyes were wet. He ran his finger over his brow, rubbing the dust away. "I thought about that day so much, wondered what would've happened if I'd been there when that animal showed up, when he threw you two in the back of that truck."

"Where did you go?" I pulled my legs in front of me

and curled into a tight ball. "What happened to you?"

Caleb rubbed his temples. "I went into the mountains. I wanted to ride until my thoughts were clear. When I came back to camp the boys were so upset. Benny . . ." Caleb sped up again, swerving around the holes filled with thick patches of weeds. "Benny was the worst."

"Where are they now?" I saw Benny's smile when he read a word correctly. Silas standing in the middle of their room, wearing his tutu, a cowboy hat cocked on his head.

"They're still there . . . with Leif." Caleb's hand returned to the wheel. Rocks and twigs plinked against the underside of the carriage. The meaning of his words sunk in. He had left behind his home, his life, his friends . . . for me.

After a long while, Caleb went on. "I'm going with you to Califia." He turned to me. "We'll get there." There was something about that word—*we*—that comforted me. There was no longer him. There was no longer me. There was us.

A life together seemed possible now. A life in Califia, this place across the red bridge, hidden in the hills by the ocean. They would take us in, this community of escaped orphans. I could teach there, Caleb could hunt and send out new messages to the boys in the labor camps. Eventually we'd return to School, as soon as we could make the journey. I'd go back for Ruby and Pip. Just like I'd promised.

I looked down at Caleb's hand, letting my fingers fall through his. They stayed there, laced together, a soothing sight. The sunlight hit the side of my face, my shoulder, my bare legs.

When I turned back to the road, my feet pressed against the floor. I grabbed at the side of the window. "Caleb! Stop!" I screamed. He braked, and my body hit the dashboard.

The car skidded to a stop. "Are you okay?" Caleb asked. I nodded, pushing myself back into the seat. I rubbed the spot where my arm had met with the hard plastic console.

"What now?" I asked, pointing straight ahead.

On the road in front of us, visible in the last of the day's light, was a van. Its tires were shredded and its windows broken. Beyond that was another car, then another, a whole line of them stretched out on the road for miles in front of us, their rusted bumpers just barely touching. The road was packed, impenetrable.

He picked up the map, looking at the thin blue line we had been following through Arizona. "This was the best route."

I glanced out the dirt-caked window to where the roadway snaked around. Ahead of us, a hundred yards away, was a pile of sun-bleached bones.

"How did Fletcher bring you here?" Caleb asked.

"I don't know," I said. "It was dark. He went over the dirt sometimes." We both got out and stood on the road, taking in the line of cars. They had been trying to get out. Whenever the plague was mentioned there was always that word: *chaos*.

Caleb moved to the back of the car, opening the trunk. He pulled out cans of food and grabbed a long tan sleeve filled with metal poles and fabric. There was a plastic tube for siphoning gas, and a metal container. Then he slammed the door shut.

"Let's stay the night here," he said, prying one of the cans open with his knife. "The troops won't find us—they'll know this road is blocked. Then tomorrow, we'll turn back, and go around the way I came. Over the mountains."

The sun was nearly down, dotting the sky with bright white stars. Back on the road, with the headlights lit, the troops would be able to spot us easily. We had no other choice.

Caleb set a tarp down beside the pavement, in a spot of

dirt half hidden by the withered, brown bushes. I watched him, his body moving silently, easily, as he drove the spokes into the ground. By the time the tent was up, the sky was gray, the moon casting a cool light on our skin.

"After you," he said, gesturing beneath the flap of dark green fabric.

The inside of the tent was just wide enough to fit both our bodies lying down. Caleb came in behind me, his T-shirt soft as it brushed against my bare arm. After days apart, the sudden closeness made me nervous.

"Well," I said loudly, every inch of my body suddenly awake, "I guess we should go to sleep now." I picked up the tattered gray blanket and folded it over my lap.

"I guess we should." Caleb laughed, his smile still visible in the dull light coming through the thin tent. "But first I have something for you."

He pulled a small silk pouch from his pocket, so dirty it could be mistaken for trash. But instantly I knew what was inside. "You left this in your room at the dugout," he said, handing it to me. "I thought it might be important."

My fingers dug into the pouch gratefully, feeling the tiny plastic bird, the tarnished silver bracelet, and finally, the worn edges of my mother's letter. "Thank you," I said, tears gathering in my eyes. He couldn't know how important it was. "I don't know how to—"

"It's nothing."

He grabbed my hand and lay down, stretching one arm underneath me so it rested in the slight space at the back of my neck. He pulled me closer, so I could feel the warmth of his body, the stubble on his chin scratching at my forehead. "Good night, Eve."

"Good night, Caleb," I said. As I listened to his breath slowing, my hand resting on his heart, the blood pulsed through my fingers, my legs, my heart. After days of wondering and imagining and wanting, he was there beside me. Three thoughts came to me in the seconds before I drifted off to sleep.

I am going to Califia.

I am with Caleb.

I am happy.

thirty-two

THE AIR COOLED AS WE DROVE FARTHER NORTH. I TOLD Caleb about the truck and Fletcher, how we'd met Lark, and the movies Otis projected on the wall. I told him about Marjorie's breakfasts of eggs and boar, and how we'd hid in that secret room while the troops searched the house. Then I told him about all I'd seen—the bullet that exploded in Otis's chest, Marjorie being struck across the cheek, the purple-red spatter that covered my legs after Lark was shot. How I made that horrible mistake. "It's all my fault. I can't stop picturing it."

Caleb pressed his lips together in thought. "You didn't know. Sometimes, in the night, I'll wake up panicked. I'll think I'm back in the labor camps—cement blocks on my back, or a boy on a cot next to me, blood and spit spilling over his lips. But then I realize it's a dream and I feel lucky."

"Lucky?"

Caleb turned to me. "Lucky that I can wake up. That now, it's only a nightmare. It used to be my life."

The car started up a steep road, its engine making a loud, grating sound under the new stress. The Sierra Nevada mountains rose around us. I stared out the window, at the steep, green hillside, and thought again of my mother, and the songs she had sung to me as she bathed me in our claw-footed tub, miming a spider with her hands.

"Do you remember your family?" I asked suddenly. Caleb had said he'd entered the labor camp when he was seven, but I knew little about his life before. Had he ridden a bike like I had? Did he share a room with brothers? Had he known his parents?

"Every day." The car stuttered as it climbed the road, slowed by the thick greenery that covered the pavement. A wall of rock rose up on one side. "I try to remember the times before the plague, when I played Capture the Flag with my brother and his friends in our yard. He was five years older, but he let me be on his team, and sometimes he'd have to carry me over the line so I wouldn't get caught." Caleb's smile appeared and disappeared.

"Where did you live?" I turned, resting my hip on the seat.

Caleb squinted. "A place called Oregon. It was colder, rainy. We were always in our jackets. Everything was so green." The car dipped into a ditch, making a scraping sound. Then we were back up, moving again, the stray plants crushed beneath the beaten tires. "What about you? Did you have any brothers or sisters?"

"It was just me and my mom." I stared out the window, at the drop-off just a yard away, its height steadily grow-ing as the car climbed into the mountains. I remembered the feeling of her breath in my ear, her fingers tickling my sides. "She used to do this thing on my birthday. She'd wake me up with breakfast and sing: 'Today, today is a very special day . . . today is somebody's birthday . . .'" Heat crept into my cheeks as I sang, my voice thin and shaky.

"When's your birthday?" Caleb drummed his fingers on the wheel, continuing the beat. "I'll remember to sing it to you."

"I don't know. We didn't have birthdays at School." All the days were the same, one after the next after the next.

I had eaten the sweet apple bread they sometimes served, secretly imagining a candle stuck in its top, just like the cakes I'd seen in those library books. "Who knows the date anyway?"

Caleb pressed the pedal below the wheel, speeding us forward. "I do."

"Oh yeah?" I smiled, not believing him. I combed my hair with my fingers. "What day is it then?"

"June first!" he said. "It's a new month." He rapped his knuckles on the wheel. "Now let's see . . . when should your birthday be? You're too argumentative to be a Sagittarius . . ."

"I am not argumentative!" I cried. "And what is a *Sagittarius*?"

Caleb smiled playfully. "Sensitive, hmm. Maybe you're a Cancer. How about something in July?"

"Why would you say I'm sensitive? What are you even talking about, *Cancer*? Isn't that a disease?"

In the late afternoon light, I could see the tiny bubbles on his nose, where the skin was peeling from the sun. "Astrology is a joke anyway, it's for the loonies." He circled his finger around his temple and crossed his eyes.

I couldn't help but laugh. "I want it to be in August," I said. "That was when School would change its schedule.

We'd begin our English courses. I always liked that month."

"Fair enough." Caleb smiled. "August twenty-eighth?"

"Sure," I said. I sat there in silence for a moment, a small, secret smile spreading across my face. After all those years of reading about birthdays in books, of seeing the pages of children blowing out cakes with candles, of being told by Headmistress Burns that School kept track of our age only—that the actual day was of no importance—I finally had one. August twenty-eighth.

The car climbed up the twisting roads, the engine groaning as the sky beyond the glass turned a flat white. It grew colder the higher we went, and we pulled the clothes from the trunk and wrapped ourselves in jackets, pants, and boots, now blanketed in the familiar smell of mildew. The sun hid behind the thick layer of gray clouds.

I studied Caleb's hands on the wheel, or the way his right foot pressed the pedal on the floor, wondering when and how he'd learned to drive. The monotonous hum of the car hypnotized me. My thoughts returned to School, to Ruby and Pip, to the long room with the beds.

"My friends are all back there, at School. There has to be some way to get them out."

Caleb scratched at the back of his head, where his

dreadlocks met the skin. He was bundled in a thick brown jacket like the one he wore the night of the raid, its collar lined with yellowed wool. "There'll be more resources in Califia. Maybe then."

He didn't say anything for a while, instead gazing through the front window at the road, which was now strewn with thin branches and dried leaves, its dirt path giving way to rocks. The car pitched and heaved on the uneven surface.

Finally he cleared his throat. "What are your friends like?"

"Pip is funny," I began. "Those first years I was in School, I was so scared the plague would come through the wall or wild dogs would get in. Everything was terrifying. Whenever I tried to complain to her she would skip off onto the lawn, dragging me with her. *Stop it!* she'd say. *You're ruining my fun!* Then she'd make a face to get me to laugh. Something like . . ." I pulled down the skin on my cheeks the same way Pip used to, exposing the red lower rims of my eyeballs.

Caleb laughed and held up his hand, blocking me from view. "Stop, please."

"And Ruby is the one to tell you if your hair looks like it's been through a windstorm, but she's also the first to yell at anyone else if they try to. Very loyal." I stared out the window. The road snaked up, up, hugging the side of the mountain until it disappeared from sight. Caleb turned the knobs for heat, fiddling with the vents, but only cold air came out.

"I know people like that. Some of my friends are still at the camps."

I was about to ask Caleb more, but the car came to a sudden halt and the air thickened with the smell of smoke. I brought it into my lungs and coughed. After a moment of confusion, our chests heaving, we finally stumbled outside.

Something in the front of the car was burning, thin gray columns drifting up from the front. Caleb waved the smoke from his face. He lifted the hood, wincing as his fingers touched the hot metal, and inspected the blackened box inside.

"It's dead," he said, coughing. He stared at the road, still twisting for miles in front of us up over a high peak, down the other side of the mountain.

The cold air chilled my bare skin. I pulled the hood of the jacket up, trying to block the wind as Caleb took the supplies from the trunk and loaded them into a backpack. "We should start moving. It'll be easier to keep warm."

I studied the map, which was crinkled and worn. It was only twenty miles over the ridge of the mountain and down the other side. "We should be able to do it in two days," I said, starting up the path. "Maybe less."

Caleb was already moving, his eyes locked on the sky. "Let's hope the weather holds." He pulled the jacket around him, tucking his bare hands beneath his arms as we began our climb. My ears popped from the height. The incline made it hard to breathe, but I kept at the path, picking up a weathered stick along the way to help me forward.

We ate cans of pineapple and pears as we went, the cold juice sliding down our throats. Caleb told me about his family: how his father had worked at the local newspaper, sometimes bringing home large boxes so he could construct make-believe houses in the backyard. I told him about the cottage with the blue shingles I had grown up in. Only I could get into the crawl space in the basement, with its thick pink fluff for walls. I told him about the day at the mailbox, my fingers gripping its wooden post as the truck came around the neighborhood. Caleb's father had gone to the pharmacy and never come back. With his mother and brother sick, he'd taken his bike through the streets, searching for his dad until the vandals came out in the dark. When he finally returned home, his family was already gone, their bodies rigid with death.

"I sat there for three days, holding my mother. The soldiers found me when they were storming houses, and they took me to the camps." My feet kept moving, climbing the steep ground beneath me, but my mind was in that house with Caleb.

We climbed in silence for a while; our fingers laced together, turning pink with the chill. We'd gone five miles when the sky released tiny white crystals. They piled up in the wrinkled folds of my jacket.

"Is this"—I held out my hand, loving the cold feeling on my palms—"snow?" I had only seen it in the distance, dusting the tops of the mountains, or in the pages of books.

Caleb glanced at the thin layer covering the road like a sheet. "It is, and it's falling fast." He kept moving, not stopping to watch.

I knew it was serious from the sound of his voice, but I just stood there, staring at the white dots in my hand. I thought of snowmen and forts and igloos, like the ones from the stories of my childhood.

Within ten minutes the wind had picked up. The flakes were thicker and fatter and piled inches on the ground.

The sweater wasn't enough, my jacket wasn't enough. The sneakers on my feet weren't enough. I felt the chill through my clothes, the wind sending my body trembling.

"We need to set up the tent." Caleb's hood blew back, exposing his hair. We pulled the fabric from its sheath, struggling to land its spokes in the hard ground. Only one went in, as the flakes blew down faster, stinging my cheeks and making it hard to see.

Caleb kept hammering one spoke with another, but the metal bent. After a long while, my body shaking with the cold, I couldn't stand it anymore. "Like this. We have to get under it now."

I pulled the fabric from the one stable rod to the ground, anchoring it with a few rocks. The back of it faced a boulder, making a small triangular space. I darted under, Caleb following close behind. It wasn't much space, but the fabric fell over the sides, giving us a little respite from the storm.

"How long will it last?" I asked. My hands were already numb. The chill reached through my sleeves.

Caleb pulled his hood up again. His hair was dusted with snow. "I don't know. Maybe the whole night." Then he pulled me toward him, tucking my body underneath his arm. His other arm wrapped around me. I immediately felt warmer, my face looking up into his.

My breaths slowed; my fear subsided; my chest no longer trembled. Caleb brought his hand to my cheek, wiping the last of the snow from my eyelashes. "Benny told me that loving someone meant knowing that your life would be worse without them in it." He smiled. "Where did he get that idea?"

My skin felt hot underneath his fingers. I smiled back at him, not saying anything.

He leaned in closer, tracing invisible lines across my cheekbones. "That's why I had to find you."

His lips pressed against mine, his arms tightened around my shoulder. I lifted my chin up, surrendering into his kiss. I couldn't stop. I thought fleetingly of the years of lessons—of Juliet's foolishness and Anna Karenina and Edna Pontellier. But for the first time, I knew:

It was all for a moment. It was all too good to be missed.

thirty-three

WHEN I OPENED MY EYES I SAW ONLY WHITE. FOR A moment I wondered if I had died and this was heaven. I lifted the section of fabric that half covered my face. The snow was still there. The ground was frozen. But the storm had cleared, leaving only the glowing sun in its wake.

I pulled myself from the battered tent. Caleb was asleep, his eyes fluttering, one arm slung over his side. Beyond the shelter, far beneath me, the world was soundless and small, a thing to be marveled at, with no guns or troops or Schools. My body hummed with the same energy as the rocks, the leaves, the sky. I was simply and impossibly free.

I raised my arms up, letting the breeze come through my fingers. I must've been there for a few minutes, when something hit me hard in the square of my back. I turned. Caleb kneeled beside the shelter, a wet snowball in his hand and a mischievous grin on his face. He threw it at me, nailing me in the neck.

I squealed and grasped at the ground, pulling handfuls of snow into my palms and packing them tight. "You're going to pay for that!" I chased him through the short trees, over rocks, nearly tripping as I pelted his back once, twice, and a third time, my steps faster with delight.

He threw another, missing me, but I grabbed his arm, pulling him down into the snow. "Uncle! Uncle!" he cried, laughing.

"Who's uncle?" I asked. I took a handful of snow and rubbed it on his neck. He twisted away, bristling from the cold.

Then in one swift motion he turned me over, his arms around me, his face pressing against mine. "It means mercy! Have you no mercy?" He kissed me again, slowly, playfully, letting my back fall softly into the snow.

—‡—

MAYBE IT WAS THE PASSING OF THE STORM, THE MOMEN-
tum of the decline, or the swell of happiness, but we
descended the mountain in less than a day's time. When
the sun lowered in the sky, we hit our first stretch of flat
road, its even mossy pavement a relief beneath our feet.

"We can stop there," Caleb said, pointing to a small
cluster of buildings about a mile off. "Hopefully there
will be something we can use for the last part of the
trek—bikes, a car, anything."

"How did you get the car anyway? That Volvo?" I asked.
I'd been so relieved to see him on the road, to feel his body
next to mine, I hadn't thought about how he'd gotten there.

A fly circled the back of Caleb's head, and he swatted
at it. He paused a moment before answering. "I traded
Lila to one of the gangs." He smiled a half smile. "They're
not bad people. Just selfish. She'll be all right."

I knew he loved that horse—it was in the way he combed
her mane or calmed her by whispering in her ear. It was how
he'd scanned the horizon that day after we'd run into the
troops, how he'd kept searching for signs of her. I grabbed
his hand and squeezed, knowing that a simple thank-you
wasn't enough. Nothing I could say would be enough.

—⊣⊢—

WE WALKED IN SILENCE FOR A FEW MINUTES WHEN Caleb suddenly stopped, his gaze settling on something on the side of the road.

"What?" I asked as he pulled my hand, taking a half step back. "What is it?"

"We have to hide." He pointed to the brush off the road, where the shrubs were flattened in two straight lines, as if smashed by tires. "It's a trap."

I turned back. The mountains reared up with nothing but grassy land between them and us. "There is nowhere to hide."

A hundred yards off, near the cluster of buildings, something moved. A figure, then two, barely visible in the dusk.

"You have reached a roadblock. You are required by law to pass through," they called through a megaphone. One of the figures raised his arm, beckoning us forward.

Caleb dropped my hand. He looked at me, back to the mountain. "Just follow my lead. Hide your face with your hair."

As we walked forward, the pack heavy on my back, I reached for the tangled mess underneath my hood, covering my cheekbones.

Three soldiers stood in front of an old shop, an AUTO

REPAIR sign hanging crooked on its front. A government Jeep was parked inside and the dusty workbenches were strewn with rusted bars, tools, and piles of cracked tires.

"We're sorry," Caleb said, averting his eyes. "It's just me and my sister. We're looking for food."

A soldier approached us. He had red hair. His eyelashes and brows were so light they gave him the hairless look of a salamander. I kept my gaze on his boots, which were shiny and black. I had never seen shoes so clean. "You went into the mountains to find food?" His hand rested on the gun at his hip.

"Through them. We came from the other side. Our house was set on fire by a rebel gang." The soldiers studied us, taking in our ripped clothes, the dirt crusted underneath our nails, the thin layer of dust that browned our skin.

"And you've obtained permission to live outside the City?" another asked. He was shorter, bulkier, his gut hanging over the belt of his pants. He rested one hand on the green Jeep.

"Yes." Caleb nodded. He'd stripped off his jacket a mile back and the collar of his thin T-shirt was now ringed with sweat. "But it was all lost."

The third soldier grabbed the packs from us. He sat in

the road and riffled through them, looking over the unlabeled cans, the tattered map, and the tent. Then he turned
to the others and shook his head. His hair was cropped
close to his skull. He was shorter and smaller than me,
his face thin.

"What are your names?" The stocky one asked. He
spoke to Caleb, but his eyes scanned my hair, the exposed
crescent of my face, and my thin, scarred legs.

Caleb stepped toward me. "I'm Jacob and this is Leah."
His voice was clear, unwavering, but the redheaded soldier kept looking at me.

Sweat slicked my skin. *Let us pass,* I thought, my eyes
on the soldier's shiny boots. *Please, let us pass.*

I listened to him breathe. Then he cracked his knuckles, a sound like snapping twigs. "Remove your shirt," he
said. I bristled, before realizing he was speaking to Caleb.

Caleb's hands rested limply at his sides. "Sir, I didn't—
I don't—" he began, his voice strained.

"Please—let us alone," I said, raising my head for the
first time. "We just need food and a good night's rest."

But the stocky one pulled a knife, a slow smile curling
on his lips. In one swift motion, he ripped the sleeve from
Caleb's shirt, exposing his tattoo.

"What do we have here?" the redhead said. He kept

his hand on his gun. "An escapee? Where'd you pick up the girl, you sorry sack?"

The one with the shorn hair stared at me. He seemed so young, a thin mustache barely visible above his upper lip. "It's her," he finally muttered. "It's the one."

Caleb charged the redhead, knocking him off balance. The younger one looked on, tentatively. The stocky soldier grabbed me around the neck and held the knife there, its cool metal pressing against my skin. The soldier breathed in my ear, the stench of alcohol on his tongue.

The redhead tumbled backward, pulling Caleb into the garage, down next to the Jeep. His head hit the bumper as Caleb grasped desperately for his gun, the soldier elbowing him.

"You morons—do something," the redhead pleaded, as Caleb came down on top of him. "Help me." Caleb was bigger than the soldier, his weight enough to pin him, momentarily, to the floor.

"Take her," the stocky one said. He pushed me onto the younger one, who hung his thin arm around my neck, holding me to his chest. His heart pounded against my back as he tried to pull me away from the men, now clustered at the Jeep's front tire.

The stocky soldier punched Caleb from behind, the

dull thud of his knuckles landing at the base of Caleb's skull. Caleb fell on top of the redhead, stunned.

"Stop!" I screamed as the biggest soldier lifted his knife. His arm moved with great fury as the blade sank into the side of Caleb's thigh.

The soldier raised his weapon again, this time pausing to aim higher, at the soft flesh of Caleb's throat. He was going to kill him.

I reached my hand to the young soldier's hip, feeling the end of his gun. There was no time. I didn't think, just yanked it from its holster and raised it in front of me, pointing at the soldier whose knife was at Caleb's neck. I stepped forward, breaking free from the boy's grip.

I pressed down on the trigger. A quick cloud of smoke expanded in front of my face. The soldier screamed as the bullet ripped through his side. Caleb rolled over, exposing the redheaded soldier, and I fired again, wincing as a bullet buried itself in his stomach.

Tears blurred my vision. I could barely breathe. Caleb grabbed the soldiers' pistols and threw them across the pavement. The redhead let out a moan, blood gurgling in his throat. And then he was silent.

Caleb tried to stand but he let out a terrible scream, the thigh of his pants a deep red. "We have to get out of here." He looked at me. Then he stumbled a few feet and collapsed, his face twisted in pain.

Beside me the young soldier had his hands up, his feet locked in place.

"You," I heard myself say. "You'll drive us."

"Are you serious?" he asked. He looked thinner now, smaller, his mouth a trembling line.

"Now." I pointed the gun at him until he started toward the car. "Now!" I yelled and he hurried to start the engine.

The soldier pulled the car out of the narrow garage. I helped Caleb in, never lowering the gun, and slammed the door.

thirty-four

"FASTER," I SAID. "YOU HAVE TO DRIVE FASTER."

My hands were still shaking. I kept the gun on the soldier as he turned left onto the cracked road marked 80. I spun around, looking out behind us for signs of other vehicles. Soon they'd be coming for us, the King's army on alert, searching for the people who had killed their men and stolen their car.

The soldier pressed down on the pedal. In the seat behind me, Caleb tried to bandage his leg. For an hour he'd applied pressure to the wound. Now he peeled the soaked pants from his skin, releasing another terrifying gush of blood.

"We have to stop the bleeding," I said, as the Jeep barreled over uneven pavement. Caleb's face had gone pale. "You're losing too much blood."

"I'm trying," he said, fastening the ripped strip of fabric around his thigh. His movements had slowed, his hands pausing on the knot, as if he needed time to think before tying it tight. "I just have to get this . . ." he trailed off, his voice quieter than before.

I could see him slipping away, each movement more labored than the one before. I rested my finger on the trigger, my attention again on the soldier. In his face, I saw the two men in the cellar, their voices calm as they searched under furniture and through the closets, looking for us. I saw them killing Marjorie and Otis. I heard the blast that took Lark, and the violent snapping of twigs as they chased me through the woods.

"I told you to hurry up," I said, my voice cold.

"I'm sorry, I'm trying," the soldier said. His foot pressed the pedal again, sending me back into my seat.

Caleb let out a low groan. His hands were covered with blood. After a long while, the soldier glanced from the gun to the road. "If we stop, I can help him."

I kept the pistol on him, afraid what he might do if I moved it away. Behind me, Caleb shook his head no.

"You're lying," I said. "It's a trap. Keep moving." We couldn't have been more than sixty miles outside Califia. We would find help when we got there. Caleb would be able to rest.

"There's an emergency kit in the glove compartment," the young soldier offered. He nodded to the small plastic drawer in front of me. "I can stitch up the wound."

"I don't trust you," I said. But behind me, Caleb was clenching his fists together, trying to steel himself against the pain.

"If I do it, you have to let me go." The soldier's gaze met mine, his eyes pleading under his thick awning of black lashes.

I looked behind me, where Caleb gripped the seat, his head back. His makeshift bandage wasn't helping. Anything could go wrong: the old tires could explode, the gas tank could empty. And if we encountered any more troops he would need his strength. Caleb's eyes closed as he drifted slowly, surely, into an unshakable sleep.

"Pull over," I said finally. "Do it quickly."

The Jeep veered off to the side of the road, stopping at a cluster of buildings. A giant, arcing yellow *M* towered above us. I got out of the car and circled it, keeping the gun on the soldier as he fumbled with the red bag from the front console. He pulled out a needle and threaded it.

There was purpose to his movements as he undid the tie around Caleb's leg. His hands stopped shaking. He stuck a needle into the wound, injecting a clear fluid. Then he pulled a piece of gauze from the bag. I hadn't seen anything so white since I left School. It was even brighter than the carefully laundered nightgowns we wore to bed.

"It's not as deep as I thought," he said. He pressed the gauze to Caleb's skin, blotting the wound, now oozing a deep burgundy. Then he cleaned the gash and stitched it shut with black thread, his eyes indifferent to the gore.

By the time he was done, Caleb's eyes were half open. "Thank you," he said.

The young man turned to me, his eyes searching mine. "Can I go now?" Tears threatened to run over his cheeks.

Caleb shook his head again. "We need him to drive."

"I promised," I said slowly. I lowered the gun. Beyond us golden hills rolled on for miles.

"We can't," Caleb said again.

The soldier clasped his hands together, pleading. "I'm going to die out here anyway," he said. "What do you want from me? I did what I said I was going to do." He looked so vulnerable, with a thin chest and legs that were all bone. He couldn't have been older than fifteen.

ANNA CAREY

I nodded to the side of the Jeep, where the road gave way to sand and shrubs. "Go," I said. "Now."

Without looking back, he ran.

"You shouldn't have done that," Caleb said. He studied the stitches in his leg. Then he adjusted himself, collapsing back into the comfort of the seat.

"He was just a boy," I said.

"There are no boys in the King's army." Caleb's skin was red from the day's sun. "Who's going to drive now?"

"I promised him," I said again, so softly I doubted Caleb had heard.

I climbed into the front seat, trying to remember how we had even gotten to this place. I turned the key the way I'd seen the soldier do. I held the wheel as Caleb had, all those miles over the desert. Then I moved the stick in the center, letting it lock on the *D*.

I lowered my foot on the pedal and the Jeep lurched forward, picking up speed, moving faster and faster toward Califia.

thirty-five

AFTER A FEW HOURS WE CROSSED AN ENORMOUS GRAY bridge and into the ruined city of San Francisco. Old, ornate houses rose around us, their colorful facades covered with ivy and moss. Cars stood abandoned in the middle of the road, forcing us onto the wide sidewalks, scattered bones crunching under the Jeep's tires. Caleb held the map, directing me over the steep hills. He coached me through each turn, each acceleration, until the road rose up and there was only a stretch of blue beside us.

"The ocean," I said. I pulled over just to look.

Below us the waves collided into one another, sloshing with white. The ocean was an expansive thing, a great reflection of the sky. Sea lions slept on a dock, their bodies slicked wet. A flock of birds circled above, greeting us with squeaky cries. *You're here*, they called to us. *You've made it.*

Caleb ran his hand over mine. His palm was still caked with dried blood. "I haven't seen it since I was a kid. My parents took us here once and we rode a cable car. It was this giant wooden thing and I held onto the side of it . . ." he trailed off.

We sat there, hand in hand, scanning the horizon. "That's it," I said, pointing to the red bridge less than a mile in front of us, stretching over the vast expanse of blue. "The bridge to Califia."

Caleb checked the map. "Yes, that's it," he said, but he didn't smile. Instead a strange expression passed over his face. He seemed sad. "Whatever happens, Eve," he said, squeezing my hand, "I just want you to—"

"What do you mean?" I glanced down at the wound in his leg. "We're here. It's going to be okay now—*we're* going to be okay." I leaned closer, trying to meet his gaze.

When Caleb looked up, his eyes were wet. "Right, I know."

"You're going to be fine," I said again, kissing his forehead, his cheeks, the back of his hand. "Don't worry—we're here. They'll help you." He offered a weak smile, then let his body fall back into the seat.

I pressed the pedal down, and we didn't stop until the sidewalk ended, every inch of the pavement now covered with cars. Caleb lowered himself from the Jeep. The color had returned to his face, but his walk had transformed into a pained shuffle, his left leg hovering just above the ground.

We started up the hill, past condemned houses and stores. Caleb's steps were tentative. He put more and more of his weight on my shoulder. I shuddered as a dark thought consumed me: what if he wasn't going to be fine? I pulled him closer to my side, as if my grasp could tether him to this earth, to me, forever.

Finally we came to the place where the bridge dug into the cliff's edge. A large park had grown over the entrance, grass and shrubs and trees spreading over the red metal opening. I pulled back a cluster of vines on the wall, exposing a plaque, greened by the years: GOLDEN GATE BRIDGE, 1937.

We reached the bridge's terrace and my heart beat faster. There was only a low guardrail between us and the three-hundred-foot drop. We maneuvered through old cars, stepping carefully onto the weeds and moss that covered the bridge.

The charred vehicles still held skeletons strapped to the front seats. A truck sat on its side, spilling out the moldy remnants of someone's apartment—broken frames, scattered books, a mattress. I kept moving, one foot in front of the other, listening to Caleb struggling for breaths.

Just as exhaustion threatened to overcome us, I looked up. There, on the other side of the bridge, high above us on a ledge in the mountain, was a stone pillar with a lantern on top. The same signal I'd seen that night in the woods when I was running from Fletcher. I heard Marjorie's voice: *If the light is on, there's room for you.*

It was the end of the Trail.

"Just a little farther," I promised, helping Caleb around a fallen motorcycle. "Don't worry." I squeezed his side in an attempt to bring him back. "Just think about how we'll be there soon. You'll be able to lie down. There'll be food. We'll eat candied potatoes and rabbit meat and wild berries, and you'll feel better after a night of rest."

Caleb held his ripped T-shirt around him, steeling himself against the wind. He nodded, but his eyes still seemed sad. I wondered if his thoughts might have taken the same dismal turn mine had.

The bridge spilled out into a thick forest. We climbed the beaten path carved out of the hill's face to where the lantern glowed through the low trees. Before us was a short stone wall. As we neared, a figure stepped out, aiming a bow and arrow at our chests.

"Who are you? What do you want?" a young woman called out. She was only a few years older than I was, her blond hair tied back. She wore a loose green dress, caked with dried mud, and tall black boots.

"We're looking for Califia," I said. I set the soldier's gun on the pavement and stepped back. "We're orphans—escapees. We've traveled far to get here. We need help."

The girl studied Caleb's leg, wrapped with the bloodied piece of fabric. She scanned his thick brown dreadlocks, the ripped T-shirt, and the pants that had been cut away around the wound. "You're together?" she asked, glancing from him to me, then back.

Behind her, an older woman appeared. "He can't come in," she interrupted, shaking her head. She had darker skin and thick black hair that bloomed in a dome around her head. She kept one hand on the knife tucked into her belt.

"What do you mean?" I asked. But Caleb was already

stepping back, lifting his arm from my shoulder.

The blond girl aimed at Caleb. "We don't let his kind in here."

"His kind?" I asked, pulling Caleb toward me. "But he's injured. He can't go back out there. Please."

The girl's face was impassive. "It's just not allowed. I'm sorry." She kept her crossbow aimed, watching us down the end of the arrow.

I held his shirt, but his hand covered mine, unfurling my fingers until there was nothing left in my grasp. "Califia has always been only women," he said, starting backward. "You go. You have to go. I'll be fine."

"You won't be fine!" I yelled, the tears hot in my eyes. "You need to come in. Please," I begged again, looking at his bloody leg, the bandage covered in dirt. The girl with the bow just shook her head.

"I knew this was how it would be," Caleb said. "Please, Eve, just go inside."

I realized then we'd never discussed what would happen when we arrived at Califia. Each time I'd spoken he'd nodded, given me a half smile, his eyes out of focus. He was taking me here, but he was never going to stay. It was only a destination off in the distance for us, never a life to be lived.

"You'll be safe there." He moved backward with

renewed strength, holding onto the tree branches as he started down the hill. The space between us grew, his steps steady as he broke us apart.

I ran after him and threw my arms around his chest, digging my heels into the ground, pulling him back. "We can live somewhere else. I'll go with you . . ."

Caleb turned around. "Where?" he asked, leaning in close, his brows knitted together. "Where is *somewhere else*?"

My throat tightened. "Maybe there's someplace on the Trail. Or we can live in the wild," I tried. "Or the dugout—we can go back to the dugout. I'll be careful."

Caleb shook his head, stroking my tangled hair. "You can't go back to the dugout. The troops are after you, Eve. They found us at the foot of the mountains and they'll find us again."

He searched my eyes until I nodded, the movement so small it was almost imperceptible. Then he kissed me, touching his lips to my cheekbones, my brows, my forehead.

I took it all in: the way the low light danced on his skin, the faint row of freckles across his cheekbones, the smell of smoke and sweat that was so distinctly him. "You'll come back?" I managed, the tears washing away the day's grit. I pressed my lips to his cheek. "Please."

"I will try," was all he said. "I'll always try."

I opened my mouth to say good-bye, but the words didn't come out. Caleb gripped my hand and pressed the palm to his lips. He kissed it and then he let go. I squeezed my eyes shut, tears rushing forward.

I couldn't say it—I couldn't tell him good-bye. When I opened my eyes, he had made it down the steep incline. His body grew smaller and smaller as he moved across the bridge.

When he was nearly across, he turned back one last time, held his arm high, and waved. *I love you*, he seemed to say, moving it back and forth until I had seen. I waved back, too.

I love you, I love you, I love you.

acknowledgments

FIRST, A HUGE THANK-YOU TO MY FRIENDS AT ALLOY Entertainment, whose faith and support has never wavered: the hilarious Josh Bank, for a lunch he didn't have to have. Sara Shandler, genius trimmer of words, for loving this from page one. To Lanie Davis, for steering me in the right direction. And to my editor, Joelle Hobeika, for all her sharp notes, her meticulous line edits, her humor and enthusiasm. You kept me tethered to the pole of sanity during those first months, when I spent more time talking to imaginary people than real ones.

I'm indebted to Farrin Jacobs and Zareen Jaffery at HarperCollins, Eve's first champions, for their continued support and editorial guidance. Another huge thank-you to Kate Lee, super agent and confidante, for all her good work.

I'm fortunate to have so many encouraging friends who celebrate my happiness as if it were their own. They deserve much more than the general thank-you I can provide here. A special thanks to the ones who lovingly read this draft when I wasn't ready to show it to anyone else: C. J. Hauser, Allison Yarrow, and Aaron Kandell. As always, gratitude to my brother, Kevin, and my parents, Tom and Elaine. I love you, I love you, I love you.

DON'T MISS THE SECOND NOVEL IN THE BREATHTAKING

SERIES!

Eve finds refuge in Califia, but she can't escape the King's soldiers forever. When she is captured and brought to the City of Sand, she learns why the King has been hunting her, and the role he intends her to fulfill. Eve feels desperate and trapped—until she is reunited with Caleb inside the city walls. Together, they will enact a plan as daring as it is dangerous. But will Eve once again risk everything—her freedom, her life—for love?

Visit TheEveTrilogy.com to follow Eve's journey.